W9-ATA-456

THE BOOK CLUB ON
WAVERLY LANE

RACHEL HANNA

CHAPTER 1

SHELBY ANDERSON WAS ANYTHING BUT A QUITTER. AS she stood in front of her new home on the outskirts of downtown Charleston, she was grateful, but nervous. After a protracted divorce and a nice financial settlement, she was finally free of the biggest mistake of her life - Roger Madden.

Her ten-year marriage to Roger had been the worst decade of her life. It had started out promising, or at least she'd thought so at the time. Her career as a real estate agent took off in her mid-twenties, and Roger had been the first mortgage lender she'd worked with back then.

They'd worked well together, and he'd made sure her deals closed. Looking back, maybe she'd fallen for him because of all the closings he'd saved for her. It definitely wasn't because of his chivalry. The man never opened doors for her or held an umbrella over her head during a rainstorm like she'd seen in the movies. Not that she couldn't do those things herself, but it would've been nice to have a man who wanted to protect her.

They'd gotten married when she was twenty-eight, and only because Shelby had given him an ultimatum - either get married or break up. She'd been ready to start a family, and Roger had seemed ambivalent about the whole thing.

They got married in the north Georgia mountains with a few friends and family members, but no kids followed. Roger had "issues" with his fertility, and Shelby felt stuck. Her parents had been married for decades, and she believed marriage was forever. The biggest contract a person ever signed.

So, she'd stayed, despite being terribly unhappy for years. It was one of her biggest regrets in life and made her feel awfully weak. Staying in a loveless marriage wasn't something she'd ever seen herself doing, but she'd done just that.

Then one day two years ago, Roger came home and said he'd fallen head-over-heels in love with his new closing attorney. She was rich, blond, and she drove a little red sports car. Shelby knew she should've been angry and upset. Instead, she'd felt free as a bird, and she couldn't wait to get out of the marriage.

Of course, by that time, they'd formed a real estate company together. All of it had to be broken apart and split between them, which took almost two years to do. Now, as she stood in front of her new stately home, she was grateful to be alone.

It seemed weird to want to be alone at her age. Forty years old wasn't exactly young, at least in her mind. She had no children, and that was a deep pain she didn't talk about often. She'd wanted to adopt at one point, but Roger had vetoed it, saying he only wanted biological kids. She'd then spent years feeling like an animal with its foot caught in a trap.

Her work with local animal rescues had kept her sane, and now that she was living in Charleston, she was sure she could find some good rescues to give her time and money to.

"All done, ma'am," the moving guy said as he walked down the front steps toward her. "We put the piano in that room on the right. Don't know what you call that room."

"Neither do I," she said, chuckling. The home she'd bought was historical, and it had lots of character. From the multiple fireplaces to the thick moldings, she couldn't wait to get it decorated. "Thanks for doing such a great job of getting me here from Atlanta. Here's your tip." She handed the man a white sealed envelope filled with cash for him and his workers.

He smiled. "Thank you very much, ma'am. Call us again if you ever need anything."

"Will do." She continued looking up at the house as he passed her and went back to the truck. The summer heat was beating down on her head as she felt beads of sweat rolling down her temples. It was late July now, and Charleston felt much like an oven. She was pretty sure she'd better get inside quick or risk cooking herself from the inside out.

"You bought this place?" Shelby turned her head, trying to figure out where the voice was coming from. It was an older woman, obviously southern. Her drawl was thicker than molasses, as Shelby's grandmother used to say. She didn't remember much else about her grandmother since she died when Shelby was in elementary school, but she remembered that phrase. "I'm over here."

Shelby turned to see the woman standing behind a large crepe myrtle tree with the biggest and brightest pink blooms she'd ever seen. Her house sat next to Shelby's, so she figured she'd better be neighborly, even though she really wanted to get inside and lay over one of the air conditioning vents.

"Oh, there you are. Yes, I'm the new owner."

The woman, who looked to be in her seventies, wore a wide brimmed straw hat with a thick pink ribbon around it, a white t-shirt, and hot pink capri pants. She was wearing gardening gloves and holding a small shovel in her hand. "You got kids?"

"No, I sure don't."

The woman stared at her for a long moment. "Why not?"

Shelby smiled. "Just wasn't in the cards for me, I suppose." She didn't like all the questions, but she was trying really hard not to start off on a bad note with her new neighbor.

The woman walked a little closer, coming out of the shadows of the crepe myrtle tree. "I never had any either. My husband was sterile."

Lovely. "Oh, well, sorry to hear that." Shelby stepped backward, trying to inch her way toward the front door.

"He died fifteen years ago. My eggs were too old to find a fertile man by then."

"I see…"

"What's your name?"

"Shelby Anderson."

"I'm Willadeene Butler. My family has lived in this area for six generations."

She seemed very proud of that, so Shelby forced a smile. "Wow. That's very impressive. If you don't mind, I need to get inside to drink some water. It's so hot out here today."

Willadeene waved her hand. "Aw, this ain't nothing. Have you been bitten by noseeums yet?"

"Noseeums? I'm not sure what that is."

Willadeene laughed loudly. "When you get bit, you'll know. Trust me. Well, I've got to get back inside. My story's coming on TV soon, and I need to make a sandwich. Do you watch Tomorrow Forever?"

"Is that a soap opera?"

"Yeah, I guess that's what they call 'em nowadays. If you get a chance, watch it. There's a man on there named River that'll make your toes curl."

Shelby almost laughed, but somehow stifled it. As brash as she seemed, Shelby liked Willadeene. "Thanks for the suggestion. I'll see you later, okay?"

Willadeene said nothing and disappeared behind the tree again. Yes, Waverly Lane was going to be an interesting place.

Shelby's first night in her new home had proved challenging. It was a historic home, but it'd been updated many times throughout the years. In fact, some of the additions and changes didn't match each other, so she'd have to get a contractor to come out and look at making things match again.

Her first night of sleep had been interrupted by several things. For one, the air conditioning unit needed help. The home was fairly large, and her bedroom was upstairs. The heat rose to the top of the house, of course, and the poor system couldn't keep up, apparently. All night, she found herself kicking off the covers and letting the ceiling fan send barely cooled air down onto her sweating body.

Shelby was fairly "well endowed" in the chest area, and several times in the night she found herself lifting "the girls", as she called them, just so the air from the fan could cool off the skin underneath them. Then it dawned on her that if she died of a heatstroke in the night, the police would find her sprawled across her bed holding "the girls" in the air. It just wouldn't make a great impression in her new hometown.

The other issue was the cacophony of sounds that plagued the night. Cicadas, crickets, and frogs seemed to sing in a chorus, and every single one of them sounded off key. She tried putting a pillow over her head, but she was so hot she couldn't do it.

Finally, after hours of trying to fall asleep, she passed out somewhere around two in the morning. Now, as she waited for her coffee pot to brew a delectable doubly caffeinated beverage to fuel her body, she wondered how she'd survive in her new house.

Maybe she'd get used to it. Surely other people heard the same sounds she did, and they were sleep-ing. Or were they? The thing was, she knew nothing about her neighbors except that Willadeene was a little odd and a lot nosy.

She'd seen other people driving down the street and some in their yards. Some smiled and waved, and some ignored her completely. Shelby had always been a social person, so she couldn't imagine living somewhere and not knowing her neighbors. What if she needed something? What if there was an emergency? Being single now, she had to think about things like that. If she fell and broke her leg, could she only rely on Willadeene? If so, she might be in trouble.

Just as the coffee finished brewing, and she was reaching for her favorite mug, someone knocked on the front door. "Of course," she muttered to herself. She assumed it was the yard guy she'd hired to take care of cutting her grass and trimming her bushes. He was supposed to come by sometime today.

Shelby walked to the door wearing her favorite silk robe and fuzzy slippers. Sure, the yard man would think she wasn't fashionable, but who cared about that?

She swung open the door to find the most put together woman she'd ever seen. The woman looked to be about her age, with long, blond hair that was as straight as a board. She had bright blue eyes, perfect porcelain skin, and bright red lipstick on her full lips. Shelby was sure she was looking at a Barbie doll come to life.

"Hey! I'm Lacy Caldwell. I live just over there in the blue house with the big azalea bushes. I wanted to personally welcome you to Waverly Lane!" Her smile was so perfect and bright that Shelby thought she might need sunglasses. How were her teeth so white? Had she never eaten anything darker than a marshmallow? Did she not exist on coffee and red wine like a normal middle-aged woman? Lacy handed her a basket with a blue and white gingham bow attached. Shelby quickly glanced at the contents and saw what appeared to be banana bread and cookies.

"Wow, thank you. Did you make all this?"

Lacy nodded, looking confused. "Of course. Why would I bring store bought gifts? I don't want you to think I'm tacky."

Shelby laughed under her breath, not sure if Lacy was being serious. "Thank you again. I really appreciate it. I haven't gone grocery shopping yet, so this might be my breakfast."

"What's your name?"

"Oh, sorry. I haven't had my coffee yet. I'm Shelby Anderson."

"Nice to meet you, Shelby. Do you have kids?"

It was the question she got asked over and over again. She'd thought about having a shirt made that said "No, I don't have kids" just so people would stop asking her.

"No, I don't have kids."

"Well, count yourself lucky. You'll keep that wonderful figure of yours," she said, smiling. "I have three kids, ages two, four, and six. Little stair steps. Nicolai is my baby, then Daphne, then Hazel." She pulled her phone from her pocket and held up a picture. Her kids looked like catalog models, each one with almost white hair, bright blue eyes, and the perfect designer clothing.

"They're beautiful," Shelby said, smelling coffee and really wanting a cup.

"So, have you met any of your other neighbors?"

"Just Willadeene."

Lacy chuckled. "She's a hoot, isn't she? I guess every neighborhood needs a nosy old lady. Oh, don't tell her I said that." She leaned back and looked toward Willadeene's house. "Wouldn't want to hurt her feelings."

"Of course not."

"We've lived here for seven years, but I have to say most people keep to themselves around here."

"Really? Most southern towns are pretty social."

"Not this street. We have festivals in town, and, of course, Charleston is full of life."

"No block parties here or anything?"

"Nope," she said, shrugging her shoulders. "But

maybe some other neighbors will come by and introduce themselves."

"I hope so. I'd really like to make some friends here. I'm newly divorced."

Lacy crinkled her nose. "I'm so sorry!"

"Don't be. I'm very happy now."

"Oh? I'd be just devastated if Ed and I divorced. I can't imagine it."

"Sounds like you have a happy marriage and a wonderful family, then." How much longer was this woman going to talk? Shelby wanted to look at her watch, but she wasn't wearing one.

"I do. I'm very blessed. Ed is an attorney, so he works long hours but provides a glorious life for our little family. I used to be an advertising executive, but I left to raise our gorgeous kids."

Something in her voice, or maybe in her expression, made Shelby think she wasn't as happy as she was making herself out to be, but that wasn't her business.

"Well, I hate to run, but I need to go get a shower and buy some groceries."

"I understand. If you need anything, even a cup of sugar, you just let me know, okay?"

"Thanks, Lacy. It was so nice to meet you," Shelby said, slowly closing the door. She peeked out the window as Lacy walked back to her house, her perfectly straight blond hair swinging back and forth like a cheerleader in high school.

"Are you sure this was the right move, honey?"

Shelby listened to her concerned mother on the other end of the line. "Mom, I told you I'm happy here. I love Charleston."

"But what will you do for work?"

Shelby chuckled. "The same thing I've been doing for all these years. I'll sign with a broker here and sell real estate."

"Ugh."

Her mother had hated that Shelby was in real estate since the day she got her license. Mona, her mother, had worried over Shelby making money because of her career being one-hundred percent commission. Mona had worked as an accountant her whole adult life until retiring last year, and she was one of the most practical people Shelby knew.

"Ugh?"

"Sweetie, you're on your own now. Selling real estate was fine when you had Roger too. But now you have to make sure you have enough for your bills. Real estate is competitive these days, so I just worry."

Shelby would've never said it, but she was worried too. Right now she was living off her divorce settlement, but after buying a house and furnishing it, she'd need to have an income pronto. Real estate was a tough job, and the market had changed in recent years, making it even more difficult. She wasn't sure how she'd break into a brand new market.

Still, when the divorce was over, she'd found herself wanting a fresh start. A new city. New people. New opportunities. Did she really want to jump back into real estate and have to start over building a name for herself? Maybe she just needed a job at the local grocery store or something.

Thankfully, the settlement had allowed her to pay cash for the house, but she still had utilities, her car payment, food, and other necessities. Surely she could make enough commission to cover those things?

"I know you're worried, but I'll make it. I promise. How are you doing?"

Mona sighed. "I'm okay. The doctor said this new medicine might make me tired, and it definitely is."

"I can come take care of you," Shelby offered yet again. Her mother had been diagnosed with an autoimmune disease two years ago, and Shelby worried about her all the time. She lived in Tennessee near much of Shelby's extended family, including her uncle, Mona's brother. He and his wife did a good job of checking in on Mona.

"You need to live your life, honey. I'll be fine with Uncle Cal. He's taken care of me since we were kids, you know."

"I know. If you ever want to come stay with me, you're always welcome."

"Thank you. Well, I'd better start dinner. I'm making spaghetti tonight." Mona was always cooking big meals even though she lived alone.

"Sounds wonderful. I could use a good home-cooked meal right about now."

"If you'd ever learned how to cook…"

Shelby chuckled. "Goodbye, dear mother."

She pressed end on the call and sighed. Growing up in the mountains of Tennessee had provided an idyllic childhood, and sometimes she missed it. Missed being near family. Missed seeing the blue-tinged mountains in every direction. Missed familiarity.

Starting over from scratch would not be easy. She could only hope it was going to be worth it.

CHAPTER 2

SHELBY LOVED HER NEW TOWN SO FAR. ALTHOUGH IT was on the outskirts of Charleston and not in the city proper, there was still plenty to do. This morning, she'd taken a long walk down the Spanish moss covered streets around her house, looking at the beautiful, stately homes and well-manicured yards. Women in spandex or yoga pants were everywhere, it seemed, and most of them had baby strollers.

She often wondered what being a mother would've been like. Would she have been strict or more lenient? Would she have played games with her kids and taken them for ice cream after school? Most of the mothers she saw this day looked pretty perfect, although she knew things were always different when people weren't on public display.

That's how it had been with her and Roger. To

everyone else, their marriage looked solid. They worked well together in business, so it would have seemed they worked well together in marriage, too. That hadn't been the case. Most nights, she was busy watching TV or taking a hot bath while Roger "worked late". Of course, working late was his way of spending time with his new love, the one who would eventually end their marriage and set Shelby free.

She could've left long ago, of course. She wasn't a weak woman. It was just familiar and easy, both things that don't lead to much personal growth. Now, as she looked at her life set out in front of her, she saw possibilities. She could do anything, quite literally.

After stopping in a coffee shop that overlooked the water, she walked down the sidewalk to a small bookstore. Tattered Pages was an adorable little shop, at least from the outside, with a bright red awning over a bay window that displayed stacks of books.

Shelby had always loved bookstores. Her love of reading had kept her sane over the years. She'd often read in the tub, of course, but also between listing appointments and real estate closings. She had a lot of downtime in her car, and escaping into the pages of a book was like a mini vacation.

She opened the heavy wooden door and immediately smelled the scent of paper. There was just something about an old bookstore, and this one was definitely old. Set in between the coffee shop and a gift shop, it was the perfect place to get out of the heat.

"Welcome to Tattered Pages. Can I help you find something?" A young, way too perky woman smiled. Her cute red bob was something Shelby could never pull off. She'd had straight brown hair her whole life. Not even a wave, no matter how humid it was. But she didn't have the petite bone structure to pull off a bobbed hairstyle either.

"Just looking. I'm new in town, so I'm checking everything out," Shelby said, smiling. She liked to wander around in bookstores. It felt like a safe cocoon that took her away from the world's problems. There was nothing more soothing than curling up with a feel-good book. She didn't care for books that made her stomach twist into knots or showered her with stress. She wanted happy endings, even if she never got one herself.

"Welcome! You can find mostly non-fiction and children's books on this level. Fiction is upstairs."

"Thank you." Shelby knew she was looking for fiction. No need for children's books, and she wasn't a huge fan of non-fiction. They taught stuff, and the older she got, the less she wanted to learn something new.

She walked up the creaky stairs, so full of character that it didn't bother her a bit. Thankfully, no one else was upstairs. Of course, it was the middle of the day on a Tuesday afternoon. Most people were at work, she supposed. Shelby had to admit, not having a job felt pretty good right now. Being a busy real estate agent back in Atlanta had taken its toll on her mental and physical health. When her divorce started, she was taking medicine for acid reflux, blood pressure medicine, and anti-inflammatories for the headaches.

Since the divorce and move, she felt pretty dang good. She was off all medication, unless she had to pop an antacid after eating something too spicy. Did she really want to go back into real estate with all its competition and worries from clients?

Right now, she decided, she would focus on finding an amazing book to read out on her new porch. It overlooked manicured gardens that the previous owners had invested a lot of money in maintaining. She figured she'd continue that with the same gardener because she knew next to nothing about growing plants. She knew how to kill them very well.

Her mother had always worried about her lack of domestic skills, insisting she needed them to get a husband. Turned out, she didn't. For all his faults, Roger was an excellent cook. When they didn't eat at home, they ordered out or went to a restaurant. Now that she was on her own, she'd have to figure out how to cook something or else risk starvation since she didn't have the funds to eat out every meal.

Shelby allowed her fingertips to touch the spines of several books as she walked down the women's fiction and romance aisles. Nothing was standing out to her today, but she rarely left a bookstore without something in her hand. Maybe she needed to jump genres and find something totally new to read. A western? Historical?

"Finding anything?" The same red-haired girl was carrying a box of books. She set them on an old wooden table next to the romance section.

"Nothing's jumping out at me so far, but I'm sure I'll find something."

"Have you read this one?"

She handed Shelby a book from the box. It had a beautiful cover with Charleston style homes on the front.

"Imogene Candler? I haven't heard of this author before."

"She's a local author, but this book took off. Hit the New York Times list, I think. She was even on CNN a few weeks back."

"Really?" Shelby turned the book over and read the blurb. It looked like women's fiction, with a bit of suspense added in for good measure. "Can't believe I haven't heard of her. Of course, I've been a bit busy lately."

"It's a great book. I've read it twice. Lots of twists and turns. In fact, I can't tell you how many we've sold to book clubs."

"Book clubs? Are there a lot of those around here?"

The woman, named Gigi according to her name tag, nodded. "A lot of women form them in their neighborhoods. I think it gives them a reason to drink wine and socialize, if you ask me. My mom's in one," she said, rolling her eyes.

Shelby laughed. Drinking wine and socializing sounded pretty fun to her. "Thanks for the recommendation. I think I'll take this one."

"Great. Let me know if you need anything else."

Shelby looked around a bit more and then wandered downstairs to the cookbook section. She was looking for easy because she had no desire to make a bunch of complicated recipes. As soon as she saw over five ingredients in a recipe, she picked up her phone and ordered a pizza.

She selected a book that said 101 Easy Recipes for Terrible Cooks, and it was like music to her ears. Thumbing through the pages, it looked like she could make many of the recipes. There was chicken salad, pot roast, and even a few casseroles that looked doable.

"Not a cook, huh?"

Shelby turned her attention toward the voice. A man who looked like he'd just stepped off the cover of GQ Magazine stood behind her. He was wearing a baby blue dress shirt, the sleeves partially rolled up his forearms, and a pair of distressed jeans that fit him like seamstresses made them while he was wearing them.

"Pardon?"

He smiled, and dimples appeared out of nowhere. She wasn't prepared for that. And he had jet black hair with bits of gray around his temples. Salt and pepper hair. Literally her dream. She wanted to rub her eyes to make sure she was awake, but thought better of it.

"Sorry. I wasn't trying to offend you. Just saw the book in your hand."

She looked down, having totally forgotten what she was doing before this godlike male appeared in her life. Maybe it was just that she hadn't dated in so long, but he seemed better looking than most of the men on the planet.

She laughed. Why did her laugh have to sound like an injured seal? "Oh, yeah. Right." *Stunning words, Shelby.*

"I'm Reed," he said unexpectedly, sticking his hand out. Now she was going to get to touch him. What a gift.

She reached for his hand. It was large and warm, and she wondered if she would feel a void when he let go. "Shelby," she choked out, acting like she'd just met her favorite teenage Hollywood crush. He let her hand go, and she felt like grabbing it again.

"Nice to meet you. Are you new in the area? I don't think I've seen you before."

"Yes, I just moved in yesterday. I live over on Waverly." *Please feel free to knock on my door any night of the week.*

"Nice area," he said, nodding his head like he was impressed. "Back to my original question, though. You don't cook?"

She felt exposed. "Not really. I'm that person who burns water."

He laughed. "Wow, that would be bad. What if I cooked for you?"

Did he just ask her out on a date? She suddenly felt like she had the world's best pheromones attracting this handsome southern gentleman. It had been a long time since she'd been on the dating scene, but apparently she was still attractive to the opposite sex.

"Cook for me?"

"Yeah, of course. Welcome you to town. Do you like braised beef tips? Parmesan mashed potatoes? Peach cobbler for dessert?"

Shelby suddenly felt like she was being punked.

She darted her eyes around, looking for hidden cameras. "Seriously?"

"Absolutely." He reached into his pocket, took out his wallet, and handed her a card. "We open for dinner at five. I recommend coming before the rush starts around six. Otherwise, it's hard to get a table."

Shelby looked down at the card and felt like an idiot. Graystone. He worked at the city's most popular new restaurant.

"Oh. Thanks," she stammered, trying to be cool but feeling massive amounts of disappointment coursing through her veins. "I'll do that."

"I'm the owner and executive chef. Dinner's on me. Just let my hostess know."

"Thank you," she said, forcing a smile and wishing one of the bookshelves next to her would open and swallow her. He wasn't flirting or asking her out. He was simply marketing his business and being nice to a new resident.

"Well, I'd better get back to the restaurant. No rest for the weary."

"Thanks for the invite," she said, wishing he'd move faster and get out of the store so she could sulk in peace.

"Have a good day," he said, raising his hand in the air and walking out. She continued with her forced smile until the little bell dinged and then allowed her face to fall. She shoved the card in her pocket, picked up her cookbook, and walked to the counter. Gigi was standing there, staring at Reed as he walked down the street.

"He's pretty hot, isn't he?"

Shelby shrugged her shoulders. "I didn't notice."

Gigi giggled. "Oh, come on. Even I can see how good looking he is, but he's kind of old. But sexy old. Like those James Bond guys in the movies. My dad used to force me to watch those. Anyway, Reed Sullivan is the most sought after bachelor around here. Never been married, but every woman is dying to date him."

"Maybe he's gay?"

"Nope. He dates women, but nothing ever sticks."

Perhaps she'd just dodged a bullet. A man in his forties who'd never been married? Wasn't that usually a red flag?

Gigi handed her a receipt and her bag. "Enjoy the book."

"Thanks," Shelby said before walking back out onto the sidewalk. Maybe Gigi had a good idea about forming a book club. Shelby needed friends. She needed to feel connected to her new community. She decided a book club was the easiest and fastest way to do that. She turned toward the print shop she'd seen on the way into town. Printing some flyers was the best way to get members for her new club, so she'd spend the next part of her afternoon doing just that.

Lacy Caldwell was anything but lazy. From the moment she woke up in the morning and her feet hit the cold hardwood floor, she was on the move. First, she made breakfast for her husband and three small children. Then, after Ed left for work, she got the kids ready for the day.

She took Daphne to preschool, and then she took Hazel to elementary school. Nicolai stayed with her while she did all the other things she needed to do. Laundry. Batch cooking meals. Volunteer work. Cleaning. She did it all, even though she could afford to hire help. Nobody did those things to her standard, so she'd given up trying to find someone.

Being the perfect wife and mother was the most important thing to her. Having been raised in a home where her father left at a young age and her mother was forced to work two jobs, Lacy had insisted upon being a stay at home mother so her kids would never think she didn't love them.

Even though she adored her babies, there were moments she didn't like to think about and certainly didn't talk about. Moments where she mourned the loss of her high-powered career as an advertising executive. Moments where she remembered her corner office with its huge window overlooking the water in Charleston. Moments where she thought about the wall of awards she'd won for advertising campaigns.

Now, she received no awards for changing poopy diapers or planning elaborate dinner parties. Her husband, successful in his own right as an attorney, insisted upon hosting a dinner party once a month for his partners and big clients. Their home easily accommodated such parties, but Lacy found it difficult to act as housekeeper and chef for the events. Sometimes, she hired a helper or two, but it was mostly her doing all the work.

On the outside, her marriage and family looked perfect. People commented on it all the time. But if they knew… really knew… what her life was like inside the walls of her huge mini-mansion of a home, maybe they wouldn't be quite so jealous. Those walls held secrets she'd never speak about in polite company. Her heart held those same secrets, and often it was almost too much to bear.

Just as Lacy was about to put Nicolai down for a nap, she heard the doorbell ring. She carried him on her hip, his little head pressed against her shoulder as he waffled between wakefulness and sleep.

"Oh, hi, Shelby. Didn't expect to see you at my door," she said, smiling broadly. Inside, she was thinking how she didn't want to see anyone right now. Her night had been rough, as it had been for over a year now, and she was looking forward to a big glass of wine after she put her son down for a nap. Day drinking was frowned upon by most people, which was why she did it in her large walk-in closet.

"Sorry to show up unannounced, but I had an idea I wanted to run past you." She stood there with an expectant look on her face, which let Lacy know she wasn't going away quickly. While Lacy loved meeting new neighbors and taking them cute little baskets of baked goods, she didn't really want them in her house. Too easy to find out those secrets best left behind closed doors.

"Come on in," she said, stepping back and pointing to her beautifully decorated formal living room. The kids weren't allowed in there because there were overstuffed white couches and hand-sewn drapes made by her great-grandmother.

Shelby walked to the sofa and sat down. "Wow. You have a gorgeous home, Lacy. Did you hire a decorator?"

She shook her head. "No. I'm a bit Type A, so I like to do things myself."

"Well, you're very talented at decorating."

"Thank you. Would you like a cup of tea?" *Please say no.*

"No, thank you. I can't stay long. I have to meet the plumber. I have a small leak under my kitchen sink."

"What can I help you with?"

"I was over at Tattered Pages today, and the young woman who works there…"

"The one with the horrible red bobbed hair and the arm tattoos?"

"Well, yes…"

She rolled her eyes. "So unseemly. Anyway, you were saying?"

"She told me that a lot of women form neighborhood book clubs around here, and I thought maybe I could do that. What do you think?"

"A book club? You mean where we read a book and then just sit around and talk about it?"

Shelby slowly nodded. "Yes, that would be how a book club works."

Lacy giggled. She knew Shelby was being sarcastic, but she decided to let it go. "Will there be food and wine?"

"I was thinking a charcuterie board, wine, and maybe a dessert. We could trade off each week."

"Weekly?"

"Well, it seems most logical. If we wait longer, we'll all forget what the book is about."

Lacy nodded. "Ah, yes. The book. I'm not much of a reader."

"Oh. I love to read."

There was a long moment of silence. "But, I suppose in an effort to get to know my neighbors and enjoy wine at the same time, I could do it. Where would we have it?" Lacy was firmly against hosting it at her own home. Dinner parties were one thing. She had control, and Ed knew the rules. But a bunch of strangers who might not want to leave at an appropriate hour? No thanks.

"We can do it at my house. I had some flyers made, so I thought I'd put them on the mailboxes up and down the street."

"Sounds like a fine idea," she said, standing.

Shelby slowly stood. "Okay, well, here's your flyer. I figure we can have our first meeting next week and choose a book."

"I'll be there with bells on!" Lacy said energetically. She walked Shelby closer to the door and opened it. "Thank you so much for coming by and inviting me to this new adventure. It'll be nice to make some acquaintances in the neighborhood."

Shelby walked out, and Lacy shut the door, sighing as she leaned against it. It wasn't that she didn't want to make friends. It was more that she didn't want to have to hide what her life had become. What her family had become. What her ten-year marriage had become.

She walked into the kitchen, grabbed her favorite

bottle of wine from the refrigerator, and headed upstairs to her oasis. As she closed the door to her walk-in closet and sat on the floor, the wine bottle between her legs and a crystal glass in her hand, she thought about how this wasn't what she expected her life to become when she was so fresh-faced and forward-thinking on college graduation day. No, this wasn't the life she'd expected, and some days she wondered just how long she could keep up this charade.

CHAPTER 3

SHELBY WALKED DOWN THE ROAD, A STACK OF FLYERS in her hand. She'd decided to wait until dusk to put them on mailboxes simply because the heat was too overwhelming during the day.

Her visit with Lacy earlier had been a little strange. She got the distinct impression that Lacy wanted her in and out of her house as soon as possible. Maybe she was just busy, or at least that's what Shelby chose to believe. She wanted to be friends with these women, and judging them before she knew anything about them wasn't a great way to do that.

"What're you doing? Handing out a petition? Is this about those speed bumps on Manchester?" Willadeene, appearing out of nowhere yet again, stood there with a running water hose in one hand and what appeared to be a can of beer in the other.

"No, not a petition. I'm forming a book club for the ladies in the neighborhood." Shelby started walking again.

"Am I not a lady?" Willadeene called loudly, annoyance in her voice. Shelby stopped in her tracks. Oh crud. Not that older women weren't invited. She didn't judge people based on age. But Willadeene? That just seemed like trouble waiting for a place to happen.

"Oh, I guess I didn't think you'd be interested."

She cocked her head to the side. "You don't think I can read?"

"Of course I know you can read, Willadeene. Here, have a flyer. We meet for the first time next week."

"I don't have to bring food, do I?"

"We'll create a schedule of who brings what once we meet. For the first meeting, I'll provide some appetizers."

"I don't eat seafood, just so you know." *She didn't eat seafood but lived near the ocean. Interesting.*

"Noted."

"I also don't eat raw tomatoes. They give me gas," Willadeene called behind her as she walked away.

"Thanks for sharing that with me," Shelby called back, making her way further up the street. She still couldn't decide if she disliked Willadeene or just saw herself about thirty years in the future.

As she walked further, she started looking at each of the houses and wondering who lived inside. Were they all happy families with two-point-five kids and a dog named Scout?

"Hey there!" She turned to see a woman standing in her yard, watering a bevy of plants, all brightly colored. Shelby wished she had such a green thumb.

"Oh, hi," Shelby said, walking over to the white picket fence.

"I'm Cami Gutierrez. And you are?"

"Shelby Anderson. I moved into the house over there."

Cami smiled, her white teeth almost blinding Shelby. She was medium height, shoulder-length black hair, and tanned skin. Shelby had always been as pale as paper, so she was jealous any time she met someone whose skin didn't appear to be almost see-through. "Nice to meet you."

"How long have you lived here?"

"Almost three years now. Wow, it doesn't seem like that long."

"Do you have a family?" Shelby hated asking if someone had kids, simply because she didn't enjoy it when people asked her that question.

"No kids. My husband is in the Marines stationed overseas."

"Really? Please thank him for his service. How long has he been gone?"

She cleared her throat. "This time? A little over two years."

"Years? Wow! I thought deployments were usually shorter than that."

Cami smiled slightly, like she couldn't say much. "He has a different kind of job that keeps him away a lot longer. We talk on video chat and on the phone a lot."

Shelby wasn't sure what to make of her answer. Maybe Cami's husband was some top secret military agent. She knew little about how the military worked.

"Let me give you one of these," Shelby said, handing her a flyer. "I'm starting up a book club, and I'd love for you to come. The first meeting will just be a get-to-know-you kind of thing. Seems like the neighbors around here are usually unsocial."

She laughed. "Yeah. Everybody keeps to themselves. I'm a friendly type, but I found out early on that not everyone feels that way. Do you do yoga?"

Shelby shook her head. "No. I tried a class once. Turns out I'm not all that flexible."

"I teach a class over at the community center on Thursday evenings. You should come sometime. It's great for stress."

"I might need to do that. I recently got a divorce

and left my profession at the same time, so I have to find a new job to pay the bills. Stress is about to become my new best friend."

"A new job? You might be interested in a business opportunity, then?"

Shelby's stomach churned. A "business opportunity" was usually code for an MLM, and she wasn't interested. She'd tried her fair share of them in her lifetime, including selling jewelry at home parties and selling vitamins through the mail. None of it made her money, and it only made her family and friends avoid her.

"I'm looking for more of a nine-to-five kind of situation."

Cami grinned. "With my company, you can set your own hours and make as much money as you want. At least let me give you a brochure. We have a great video presentation on our website." She ran to her garage and took a brochure from a box before running it back to Shelby.

Shelby took it, unable to say no. She glanced at it and saw it was a company selling all kinds of crystals and New Age products. Definitely not Shelby's thing.

"Thanks. And I do hope you'll come to the book club. I need some friends around here."

"Me too," Cami said, laughing.

"I'd better keep putting out these flyers. I'll see you around!"

"See ya!"

Hunger was a powerful thing. As Shelby stood in front of her mostly empty refrigerator and even more empty freezer, she realized what she needed to do most - go to the grocery store. She kept meaning to do it, but instead she'd managed to go to the bookstore and hand out flyers in her neighborhood. Now that she'd walked what seemed like ten miles, she was starving.

It was late, so going to the store now seemed like a monumental task. All she had in her fridge was half a carton of eggs and almond milk. That didn't seem like a great dinner. She continued staring into the refrigerator and allowed the cold air to hit her as long as possible until she finally closed it.

Thankfully, she knew there were restaurants around that offered takeout, and that was a good thing because she was a gross, sweaty mess. No use in taking a shower before eating some dinner. She'd probably pass out from starvation if she did that.

Perusing her phone, she looked at her local restaurant options. The closest one was a place called Pogo. She could get some chicken fingers and fries there, slink back home, shove them into her face, and take a nice hot shower. It was the little things in life.

She hopped into her car and drove around the corner and down the street, parking in front of Pogo. Her mouth was watering as she thought about those chicken fingers. As she approached the door, she saw a big yellow sign on the glass. CLOSED.

Closed? It was only eight o'clock. A man came out from behind the restaurant. "Can I help you?"

"You're closed?"

"Yes, ma'am. There was a water main break earlier. We can't use the water yet, so we're out of business. The only place open is Graystone, those lucky dogs. They weren't affected." He continued walking and got into his small compact car.

Graystone. Absolutely not. No way was she going there and possibly running into that godlike man again. She looked like a troll that lived under a bridge… and sweated a lot.

But she was so hungry. Not hungry enough to drive across town to the nearest grocery store, apparently, but hungry nonetheless. She got back in her car and drove around the corner to Graystone. The place was busy since it was the only restaurant open for miles around. She finally found a parking place near the back by the dumpster. Shelby sat there for a few moments, trying to figure out how to get in and out without being seen by Mr. Hot Stuff.

She quickly ordered on the mobile app and sat there for another fifteen minutes. She figured that was plenty of time to get her chicken fingers and fries in a bag. Her plan was to run in, get her food, and get the heck out of there in record time.

As she approached the door, she saw a teenage girl standing at the hostess desk and a line of brown paper bags lined up on the shelf behind her. Surely one of those was her delectable meal, probably prepared by the male model himself.

Having ordered from the kids' menu, she certainly didn't want him to see that instead of getting one of his prize winning meals, she got chicken fingers like a toddler.

"Hi, I'm here to pick up an order..." Shelby said as the teenage girl waved across the restaurant. Before she knew it, the girl was gone, and Shelby was left to stare at the bags of food in front of her. One of them had to be hers. For a moment, she considered sneaking behind the stand, opening each bag, and sniffing out her chicken fingers, but she refrained.

"Hello again." Oh no. His voice. She'd know it anywhere. Deep, dark, rich, thick, southern. She turned her head and looked up at him.

"I'm here to pick up my order," she blurted out.

"I see that. Looks like Katie is busy with a customer. Let me look. Shelby, right?"

"Right," she said, wanting to fall to the floor and crawl out of the restaurant. She was wearing a pair of ratty jean shorts, a distressed white band t-shirt and sneakers with no socks. Everyone else in the restaurant looked like they were going to the local nightclub or to church with their grandma.

"Chicken fingers and fries?" he asked, confirming her order.

She nodded. "Yes, that's me. A big child."

He smiled. "I don't judge what people eat. I just want the food to be good, whether it's chicken fingers or filet mignon." He handed her the bag.

"Thanks," she said, taking the bag. There was a lingering moment where he was looking at her, but saying nothing.

"Can I ask you something?"

"Sure."

"Back at the bookstore, did you think I was asking you out on a date?"

Her face burned, and she knew her pale skin was betraying her as it turned redder and redder. "No, of course not."

He chuckled. "I thought back on that conversation and realized later how it sounded. I'm so sorry if I gave you the wrong idea."

She wanted to throw up, but there was nothing

in her stomach. Maybe later, after the chicken fingers.

"No apology necessary. I didn't think that at all."
Lies, all lies.

"Good. I just really like to invite newcomers to Graystone. I think we have a great place here. I hope you'll come dine in sometime."

"Of course."

Maybe he was gay. Or dating some other attractive woman who looked like she belonged on the cover of a lingerie catalog. Or maybe he just found her revolting in her post-sweaty-mess attire. Regardless, she just wanted to escape the situation and stuff her face.

"Well, have a good night," he said, holding up his hand and walking away as Katie returned.

"Did you need something else?" Katie asked.

Shelby realized she was frozen in place and staring as Reed walked away. "Um… yeah, actually. Do you have honey mustard?"

"It's in the bag," Katie said, looking at her funny.

Shelby looked in the bag and giggled. "I was just testing you. You passed!" Without looking at Katie again, she slipped out of the restaurant and into the safety of her car. When did she become so awkward?

Cami sat by the phone, just as she did most nights of the week, hoping to hear from her husband. He'd been away so long, and it was pure torture for her to be alone. She'd never enjoyed being by herself.

As a kid, her mother worked a lot and her father was never in her life. That meant long nights alone as a "latch key" kid. She let herself into the house after school, made a snack, did her homework, made her own dinner, and often she put herself to bed. Her mother would come in after midnight from her shift at her second job and kiss her forehead. Sometimes, Cami had tried to stay awake long enough to feel her lips on her forehead, but often she slept through it.

Most mornings, her mother was there, which was probably why mornings were still her favorite time of the day.

She loved sitting with her mother while she made both of them French toast or those frozen waffles with the little blueberries inside. Those were simpler times, and right now Cami sure could use the warmth of her mother.

Unfortunately, she had passed away about ten years ago after a brief but violent battle with cancer. And now that her husband was gone, Cami felt more alone than she ever had. That's why when the neighbor suggested a book club, she thought it might be a good thing for her.

Of course, she had some friends at work, but they weren't exactly the most exciting people. She much preferred selling her products, but unfortunately, that business hadn't taken off enough to support her just yet. She was working hard at it while also teaching yoga classes on the side. Much like her mother, she was a hard worker.

She was happy to live in such a nice home, although she was very different from everybody else in the neighborhood. Having grown up poor, she knew the value of a dollar. She understood hard work. And it was only because she and her husband had worked so hard that they had been able to afford this house in the first place.

With him gone, much of the expenses fell on her. Between her job at the pediatrician's office, her side business and teaching yoga, she could pay her bills, and right now that was about all she could ask for.

She bit into her grilled cheese sandwich and stared down at her phone. It was nights like these that she wanted to talk to her husband so badly, but she had to wait for his call. He couldn't just pick up the phone any old time, and she certainly couldn't reach him directly.

It was hard. She had no kids, no extended family. She didn't even really know her neighbors after all these years. Everybody kept to themselves on

Waverly Lane, at least until this new neighbor moved in.

Maybe she could become friends with Shelby, she thought. It was hard to be friends with people when you were keeping a secret, though. How could you really show them who you are without being honest?

Before she could think about it too deeply, her phone rang. She practically jumped out of her skin as she grabbed it, only to realize it was a scam call. Dominic rarely called after nine o'clock, and when she noticed it was nine-fifteen, she knew she would not hear from him tonight.

It had been almost a week since she had heard from him last. She was worried about his safety. Sometimes it was hard to sleep because it was all she could think about. What if somebody hurt him?

She leaned back against the sofa, remote control in her hand. The only thing to do when you can't stop thinking about something is to watch useless TV, eat a grilled cheese sandwich, and cry.

CHAPTER 4

SHELBY DIDN'T KNOW WHY SHE WAS SO NERVOUS. IT wasn't like she was hosting the Oscar's or having the Queen over for dinner. It was just a few ladies from her new street. So far, she knew Lacy and Cami were coming, and she'd heard from another woman named Joan that she hadn't met at all. Didn't know a thing about her. There were some other "maybe" responses, so she hoped there would be at least five or six people there.

She finished laying out the snacks, which consisted of a charcuterie board because it was "in fashion" to do those now. She had wine, coffee, shrimp and a few other things to hopefully make her look like a good hostess.

As she was putting the finishing touches on her spread, the first doorbell ring startled her. She walked over, took a deep breath, and opened it. Willadeene stood there with a plate of something in her hand, a giant hat on her head, and a scowl on her face.

"Well, are you gonna let me in or just stand there?"

Shelby opened the door further and stepped back. "Come on in, Willadeene. What do you have there?"

She pushed the plate toward Shelby. "Deviled eggs. They have sweet pickles in them, like God intended. Where do I sit?"

Holding the plate of deviled eggs that didn't even remotely go with the other food, Shelby pointed toward the living room. "You're here first, so you can pick anywhere you'd like."

Willadeene plopped down in the armchair near the window, letting out a simultaneous grunt and sigh as she did. Shelby didn't know what to make of this woman. Sometimes, she was entertaining, and other times, she was annoying.

"Knock, knock," Cami said, poking her head through the still cracked front door.

Shelby smiled. "Come in!"

Cami handed her a bottle of wine. "I figure you can never have too much."

"Very true. Have a seat in the living room. Willadeene is already in there."

Cami's eyes widened. "Willadeene is joining book club?" she whispered.

"She saw me putting out flyers and basically invited herself. I figured what harm could come from inviting a lonely old woman to book club?" Shelby said, shrugging her shoulders.

"That lonely old woman is the neighborhood gossip. She's just here to get dirt on everyone, not to be a good book club member. Watch out for her."

"Well, I don't have any dirt for her to get, thankfully," Shelby said, laughing as Cami walked into the living room.

One by one they arrived, each of them bringing something for the get-together. Lacy brought French macarons that she'd made herself. Joan, who she finally met, brought cucumber finger sandwiches. Shelby had never had those, but had seen them in movies where people had tea in fancy places.

Joan was interesting. From what she could gather, she was a widow and had a grown son living somewhere else. Other than that, she seemed nice enough, although quiet. She didn't seem to know anyone on the street either, which Shelby found so odd.

There were a few other women whose names she was trying to keep straight in her head. Sylvia? Dalia? She wasn't totally sure, but she'd figure it out soon enough.

"I wanted to say thank you all for coming," Shelby said, standing in front of the group like she was giving an oral book report in eighth grade. "Being new in town, I was looking for a way to make some friends and get to know my community. Gigi at Tattered Pages gave me this idea for a book club, so I hope we can do this together."

"Gigi looks like a weirdo," Willadeene blurted out before taking a long swig of her wine. Shelby continued.

"Anyway, Gigi also told me this book is very popular with other local book clubs." She held up her copy of the book. "It's about a woman whose husband dies and leaves her not only in debt, but without a home. Seems really interesting."

"Or depressing," Willadeene muttered under her breath.

"My friend told me it's a great book. Lots of twists and turns," Lacy said, smiling. "I'd love to read it."

"I thought we could do two to three chapters a week? Does that sound doable?"

"I think so," Cami said, nodding. "And we'd meet every week?"

"Yes. We can meet here each time, or we can change houses if y'all would prefer that."

"I think meeting in the same place each week makes more sense," Lacy said.

"Great. We can create a sign-up sheet for who brings what each time. Maybe we can even do some theme nights? You know, like a taco bar, dessert night, stuff like that."

Shelby loved how it was all coming together. Everybody seemed super nice, but nobody was really interacting with each other. She hoped that would get better as time went on.

After the meeting was over and they'd planned how to get the books and when the next meeting would be, Shelby mingled around her living room and kitchen, getting to know everyone. Joan, the widow, seemed very shy but nice. She had a grown son who lived in Utah, but she said they didn't talk much. Shelby wondered why, but didn't ask.

"Great meeting," Cami said, handing Shelby a glass of wine.

"Thanks. I think this will be fun."

"Totally. I'm getting my book tomorrow so I can start reading this weekend."

"I've already started reading, and it's great."

"I know you said you wouldn't be interested in a business opportunity right now, but…" Shelby wanted to correct her and say, *"I'm not interested in your business opportunity or anything that involves recruiting other people,"* but she refrained. "But we have a big bonus right now where you can get five percent more on your sales if you sign up for our new business owner package. It's an amazing deal!"

Shelby almost felt sorry for her. She knew Cami was just trying to make ends meet like everyone else, but she didn't know how many other ways to say she wasn't interested.

"I appreciate you thinking of me, but I'm just not interested in running my own business."

Cami stared at her. "Didn't you say in your introduction that you were in real estate for years and ran a business with your ex-husband?"

Shelby smiled. "Well, yes…"

"This wouldn't be much different except for no horrible ex to deal with. Come on! Just watch the video presentation. I think you'd be a great fit or else I wouldn't even mention it."

"Are you trying to recruit Shelby into a pyramid scheme?" Lacy asked, walking up next to them.

"We don't call it that," Cami said, obviously offended. "It's an actual business."

Lacy rolled her eyes. "You can call it a pyramid scheme, an MLM, or a business opportunity. All of it means the same thing."

"Ladies, let's not argue," Shelby tried to say.

"You know, I don't remember anybody asking your opinion," Cami said, standing up straighter. Shelby worried they'd have a brawl right there in her living room.

"We're at a social function, dear. Anyone can talk to anyone. Besides, I wasn't trying to be rude. I was just warning Shelby."

"I was talking to her about my business. What do you do for a living?" Cami asked, crossing her arms.

Lacy cleared her throat. "I'm a homemaker. It's the most important job in the world."

"Shelby, I wanted to thank you for such a nice get together," Joan said, appearing next to them as if she was an angel sent by God. She distracted Cami and Lacy enough from their argument to make it stop.

"You're very welcome. Will you be joining book club?"

"Absolutely. It's been a long time since I've had a social life. Since losing my husband, it gets lonely over in that big house."

"How long ago did you lose him?" Cami asked.

"Almost six years now. It was very sudden. A work accident."

"Well, I hope you sued the pants off his employer," Lacy said, pursing her lips.

"They paid a settlement," Joan said, her voice small and quiet.

"Good! I know it didn't bring your husband back, but at least you have that money to fall back on for the rest of your life."

Joan's eyes darted around uncomfortably. "Well,

I'd better go. I need to take my dog for a walk before bed."

"It was so nice to meet you, Joan. Did you put your phone number on the sign-up sheet?"

"Yes, I did."

"Great. I'll text everyone tomorrow with our first meeting day and time."

Joan smiled and nodded as she turned toward the door. There was a deep sadness about her. Of course, she'd lost her husband, but there seemed to be more to it.

"That's one strange lady," Willadeene said, walking up and interjecting herself into the conversation.

"I thought she was very nice," Shelby replied.

"She's a widow. I think she's just lonely," Cami said.

"I'm a widow, and I'm not weird." Shelby begged to differ, but she wasn't going to say that out loud.

"Can we agree book club is a safe place for all of us to be ourselves, warts and all?" Shelby suggested. Willadeene rolled her eyes.

"You're not one of those people, are you?"

Shelby put her hand on her hip. "What people?"

"I think they call them snowflakes."

"Okay, okay. I think that's quite enough," Lacy said. "I think Shelby is right. Book club should be a place where we can all talk openly and form bonds with each other, no matter how different some of us might be." Lacy cut her eyes to Willadeene and then back to Shelby as she stifled a smile.

"I'm going to need a ride to the bookstore to get my book. I hate going in there with that weird red-haired girl," Willadeene complained. At least she'd changed subjects. Cami, Shelby, and Lacy all looked at the other, trying to figure out who'd be the unlucky one to take Willadeene.

Shelby sighed when it was clear the other two women weren't about to put her in their vehicles. "Fine. We'll leave at ten tomorrow morning. Meet me in my driveway, okay?"

Willadeene picked up her oversized floral purse and slung it over her shoulder. "Okay, but you should know I don't like the car too cold. And I don't listen to rap or country music." She marched toward the door and then turned around. "I have to take my pills at eleven, so you should plan on eating lunch with me."

"I'm very busy, Willadeene. Can't you just eat a snack before we leave?"

She shook her head. "I'll be hungry by eleven." She shut the door behind her and Shelby stood there wondering what in the world she'd gotten herself into.

∾

Joan McClendon didn't recognize her life anymore. When she'd moved to Waverly Lane with her husband, Andrew, nine years ago, they'd had such big plans. He was an antiques dealer who traveled all over the world to find the perfect pieces for his wealthy clients. Vases from France, bronze statues from Italy, furniture pieces from the remotest of places all over the world. He was like a private investigator for the past, and Joan had always admired him for that.

She, on the other hand, had never followed her passions. She'd worked as a teacher for most of their marriage, leaving the field behind after he died. Her sorrow and grief had been too much, causing her to break down in front of thirty second-graders one day. She'd known it was time to leave that life behind at that point.

Since then, she'd become so reclusive, almost like a hermit. That's why the invitation to book club had been so hard for her. Saying no meant continuing to live a life of loneliness. Her only son, Paul, lived in Utah and hadn't spoken to her in years. His grief had been huge when he lost his father, but his disappointment with her was the straw that broke the camel's back. She couldn't blame him; she was disappointed in herself.

Shaking off the overwhelming barrage of feelings, she picked up the picture of Andrew she kept on her nightstand and ran her index finger across his cheek. Their marriage had been one for the ages. Romance from day one that didn't stop until he took his last breath. Andrew had allowed her to be who she was, and she'd adored him for it.

Now in her sixties, she wondered what the rest of her life would be like. Losing him so suddenly had rocked her in ways she couldn't describe. She knew she needed counseling, but she'd never gone. There was this irrational fear that if she worked through the grief of losing her soulmate, she'd also lose the feeling of love she still held for him. That she couldn't bear.

Telling people he died in a work accident had always been easy. Explaining that Andrew, the love of her life, had also been a raging alcoholic for most of his adult life and that he drank himself to death was a much harder story to tell. She didn't like to think of that part of him. She didn't like to remember the day she found him. Those memories were fuzzy and foggy, and she was thankful for that much.

"I miss you so much," she whispered, kissing his picture as she did every night before bed. She set it back on the nightstand and slid under the covers, her eyes welling with tears.

Six years. To most, it was a long enough time to grieve and move on. But each one of Joan's days was a long slog through grief that no one else saw. Her grief was evident in every part of her home, but no one ever came inside to see it. She lived in her own world of hidden shame, and she would likely die there.

Closing her eyes, Joan didn't dare dream of better days. There were none to be had, as far as she was concerned.

Shelby stood in the bookstore yet again. This time, she didn't go upstairs at all, even though she wanted a new crime novel to read. Nope. Today she was looking for a book on how to write a good resume. She'd never had to create a resume, so this was unfamiliar territory for her. She could've looked for the information online, of course, but any reason to go to the bookstore was a good enough reason for her.

Thankfully, Willadeene had woken up with a headache, so she decided not to go with Shelby to the bookstore. Instead, Shelby offered to pick up the book for her.

"Hello, again!" Gigi said as she walked in the door. Shelby noticed a big cardboard box on the counter.

"New shipment? Anything good?"

Gigi smiled. "Not a shipment, actually. Those are my personal things."

"Your personal things?"

"I didn't have an office here, but I kept some stuff around since I was here a lot. My coffee maker, my teapot, picture of my boyfriend," she said, looking inside.

"You don't work here anymore?"

"Not after today," she said, sticking out her lower lip.

"I'm so sorry to hear that. Can I ask why?"

"My boyfriend and I bought a van, and we're going to travel the country so he can busk."

"Busk?"

Gigi giggled. "He sings and plays guitar on the street for money."

"Oh. Sorry. I didn't know there was a specific name for that." Shelby felt so out of touch. "What will you do?"

"My art. I paint and make things with mixed media. I hope to do some traveling shows."

She had to admire the girl. She was chasing her dreams at a young age, even if they didn't make sense to other people. It was brave.

Shelby figured what she was doing - starting over in a brand new town - was pretty brave too. Even though she tried to have a positive attitude, sometimes it was difficult to think about how her life had turned out so far. Divorced. No career. No friends in her new town - yet.

"Well, good luck to you! You're young and courageous to live life on your own terms. I'll miss seeing you here even though we just met," Shelby said, smiling.

"My grandma owns this place. If you know of anybody looking for a job, tell them to come apply. She's pretty picky, and she needs somebody reliable."

The wheels in Shelby's brain started turning. Would it be weird for a forty-year-old woman to give up a successful career in real estate to work at a mom-and-pop bookstore? She needed a break from the hustle and bustle of selling houses, and she'd always dreamed of working at a bookstore, as weird as it sounded when she thought about it.

"What about me?" she said without thinking.

"You? I didn't realize you were looking for a job."

"I mean, I've been in real estate for years, but I'm a little burnt out. Since I'm new to the area, it would take a while to build a name for myself here. I need a job, and I love books."

Gigi smiled. "If you want, I can recommend you to my grandma."

"That would be great! Here's my number," she said, writing it down on a piece of paper near the register. "She can call or text me anytime."

She laughed. "Grandma doesn't know how to text. She's not great with technology."

"No problem. She can call me then."

"You know what? She's just down the street at the cafe. Want me to see if she can come meet you after she finishes her lunch?"

"I would love that," Shelby said, suddenly feeling nervous. It wasn't like she was interviewing for some prestigious job. It was a cashier job at a bookstore, but to her it felt very important right now.

Gigi took out her phone and called her grandmother while Shelby wandered around the front of the store like a lost puppy.

"Hey, Grandma? Listen, I have a lady here who wants to meet you about taking over my job. She's new in town and a regular customer… Uh huh… Okay, we'll see you then." She pressed end and smiled at Shelby. "She's paying for her food and then will be on her way."

"Great. I'll just go look around at the cookbooks."

CHAPTER 5

SHELBY WALKED AROUND IN THE COOKBOOK SECTION, trying to find something as remedial as possible. She liked the cookbook she had purchased a few days before, but now she was looking for something that was even more basic.

She thumbed through a couple of books until she heard the little bell ding on the front door of the bookstore. Turning around, she saw something she couldn't believe she was seeing.

When Gigi said her grandmother was coming, she didn't expect to see a woman who looked virtually the same as her granddaughter, only about fifty years older.

"How was lunch?" Gigi asked, hugging her grandmother. The woman looked like she stepped right out of a tattoo parlor that was next-door to a hair salon. She had spiky red hair, earrings lining each earlobe, and she was covered in tattoos. Shelby had never seen someone in her age range look like that.

"Oh, it was good enough. I swear, those people don't know how to make a Reuben to save their lives."

Shelby stood there, like a deer in the headlights, staring at the woman. It probably wasn't the best way to get a job, but she was just so dumbfounded. Not that she had anything against piercings or tattoos or crazy hair colors, but she sure didn't expect to see it on someone who had to be pushing seventy years old.

"Grandma, this is Shelby. She is the one who's interested in working here," Gigi said, smiling as she pointed in Shelby's direction.

The woman eyed her carefully. "Well, are you going to keep standing over there, or are you going to come closer?" she said, putting her hands on her hips. "You have to be able to greet people if you're going to work here, dear."

Shelby shook her head slightly and laughed. "I'm sorry. I was just not expecting…"

The woman smiled. "Don't worry. Most people aren't expecting me. The world thinks I'm supposed to be old and feeble and gray-haired. Maybe I should get a walker and put sequins all over it. Or join water aerobics down at the YMCA."

Shelby held up her hands. "I didn't mean that."

"It's okay. Everybody thinks Grandma looks crazy. She's used to it. And don't let her ornery attitude get to you," Gigi said, lightly slapping her grandmother on the shoulder. "She likes to mess with people."

"I'm Ginger. It's nice to meet you, doll," she said, holding out her hand. She had rings on almost every finger and bright red nails. It seemed like every inch of Ginger's body was decorated.

"It's very nice to meet you. I love your bookstore."

She looked around at the shelves. "I love it too. It's been in our family for four generations now. I hope it continues for many years to come, but this one over here wants to go experience a little traveling."

"I've told you for years that I was leaving one day, Grandma. I'm not interested in running a bookstore. It's just not my thing."

She put her arm around Gigi. "Well, I'm a big believer in finding your thing."

"She's very brave to go out into the world and chase her dreams," Shelby said.

"Well, we can agree on that."

"You said four generations, so does that mean that Gigi's mother also works here?"

Gigi's smile disappeared. "Actually, my mother left when I was a little kid. My grandma raised me."

"I'm so sorry. I shouldn't have asked."

"What doesn't kill us makes us stronger," Ginger said. "Except for sharks and bears. They will definitely kill you."

Gigi laughed. "Well, I guess I will let you two talk. Good luck, Shelby."

"Come on into my office," Ginger said, walking toward a door across the room. She was wearing a pair of distressed blue jeans with fringe on the bottom, some slip-on high-heeled sandals that were making a noise as they clomped against the hardwood floors, and a white blouse that had sleeves that could only be described as bat wings.

Shelby found a chair across from a small desk. The room wasn't that big, and there were books lining all the walls. She felt a bit claustrophobic. She noticed some framed pictures on the walls of what appeared to be different family members, all of them standing in the bookstore at different times in history.

"This is an amazing building."

"Yeah, my dad bought it with the money he inherited from his grandfather. He was the first entrepreneur in the family. That's him up on the wall."

"He was handsome," Shelby said.

"Yes, he was. When I got old enough to understand how to work a cash register, he pulled me in to work with him. Me and my brother worked many hours in the store growing up. My brother got killed in a farming accident right after high school, so it fell to me to take the place over when my dad got too old."

"I'm so sorry for your loss."

"Yeah, he was a good brother. I miss him still. Anyway, when I got married, I ran this place with my husband. We had our daughter, but she was never much interested in working here. She wasn't much interested in anything that wasn't drugs and alcohol, unfortunately."

Shelby didn't know why this woman was telling her all this personal information, but she couldn't help but be interested. She had always loved gossip, as long as it wasn't about her.

"Well, I'm glad Gigi had you to take care of her."

"I never thought my daughter would leave her baby girl like she did, but she left. Never came back. Haven't heard from her in almost sixteen years. She sent a few cards the first few years, but then she disappeared. I don't even know if she's still alive."

"That had to be hard on you and Gigi."

"It was. It still is. A girl needs her mother. Do you have a mother?"

"I do, and I'm close to her. She worries about me."

Ginger chuckled. "As mothers always do."

"Very true."

"Do you have kids?"

"I don't. I was never blessed with them."

"A husband?"

"Nope. Recently divorced."

"Good."

"Excuse me?"

"Then you won't be distracted. Seems like you could work a lot of hours?"

She nodded. "Oh, yes. Of course. I had a really successful career in real estate, but that wasn't here in Charleston. It would take me a long time to rebuild a reputation in a whole new city, and I am kind of burnt out with the business, to be honest."

"Well, I need somebody I can trust. Somebody who will be nice to my customers. Somebody who loves books."

"I am all three of those things," Shelby said, smiling.

Ginger looked at her for a long moment. "You know what? You seem like good people. I'm gonna take a chance on you."

Shelby smiled. "Really? That's very exciting. I've always wanted to work in a bookstore."

"I hope you can lift heavy boxes?"

"If the boxes are full of books, I can certainly do that."

∾

Lacy stared down into the large pot cooking on the stove. She spent so much of her life preparing food. Presenting food to guests. Cleaning up after people ate food. The irony was, she didn't eat much. Her doctor was worried she was underweight, but Lacy didn't care. Looking svelte and fitting into her small sized clothes was much more important than meeting some random number on a chart in her doctor's office.

Tonight was another dinner party for Ed's associates. She took this part of her job as a homemaker very seriously. She was known for throwing the most lavish parties, and her food was always talked about for weeks after one of her soirees. Her whole life she'd dreamed of being the house everyone wanted to come to, and that they would talk about how good of a cook she was. She wanted to be admired, although she'd never admit it out loud.

"People should start arriving in about half an hour," Ed said, breezing into the kitchen. Sometimes she looked at him and remembered those early days of their courtship. He was tall, lean, and blond, just like their children. She remembered when they would go see movies together, take long walks by the water, and go on exciting trips. It'd been a long time since any of that had happened.

"Good. The soup is almost done. The prime rib is ready. The salad is in the refrigerator."

He rolled his eyes and laughed under his breath. "You don't have to rattle off a checklist to me, Lacy. I trust everything will be perfect as it always is." He took a grape from the fruit bowl on the counter and popped it into his mouth.

"The kids are with Annika, in case you were wondering."

He stared at her for a moment. "I figured that."

Annika had been their longtime babysitter. An older woman, she lived a few blocks away, closer to the water. Lacy had met her before she even had kids when they'd worked together in advertising. Now that Annika was retired, she loved to spend time with Lacy's kids since she had no grandchildren of her own.

"I noticed you were in my hobby room this morning."

"I was looking for my stapler."

She turned and looked at him. "Ed, you know my hobby room is off limits. We've discussed this."

His nostrils flared. "And you know to keep that door locked. What if Hazel wandered in there? She could find…"

She held up her hand. "Stop. Hazel's not old enough to know what she's looking at, and I keep the door locked."

"Well, it wasn't locked this morning, Lacy. How else could I have gotten in?"

She turned back toward the sink, where she was rinsing a measuring cup. "I don't need you checking behind me. I'm a grown woman, after all."

"I don't want my kids to know…"

Just then, the doorbell rang. Lacy's face automatically shifted into "good hostess" mode as she dried her hands, pasted on a smile, and headed toward the front door. It was time to do what she did best - play pretend.

Shelby stood behind the counter, her fingers poised over the cash register. After just two days of training with Gigi, she was alone to man the store for the next few hours. Ginger was on speed dial, of course, but other than that lifeline, she was on her own.

Gigi had left for her traveling adventure, so Shelby couldn't call her. She'd taken a ton of notes during training, so hopefully those would hold her in good stead.

"Let me know if you need any help," Shelby said, smiling at a customer who walked in. She turned back to the register and looked down at it. Why did it seem so much more complicated than the ones she'd worked with as a teenager, back in her days of working in retail and fast food?

Finally gathering her courage, she walked out from behind the counter and straightened some books on a nearby shelf. She liked order, and books sticking out drove her nuts. The woman who'd just come in wandered back out, and she was alone again.

She walked over to the stereo system and changed the music to something a little more festive. She loved eighties music, and when her favorite Michael Jackson song came on, she couldn't help but get lost in the rhythm. She took a cleaning cloth and started to clean the wooden handrails going up the staircase. God only knew what germs people had on their hands.

She shimmied and shook as she walked up and down the stairs, occasionally kicking her leg and leaning her back against the railing for effect. Thank goodness there were no cameras in the store. Ginger said she didn't believe in those "creepy things".

Suddenly, she heard someone clear their throat. She turned and looked down at the bottom of the stairs. Reed Sullivan. How did she have this uncanny knack for looking stupid in front of this man? First, with her book choice. Then, with her sweaty restaurant appearance. And now with her horrendous dancing skills that probably resembled that of a drunk walrus.

"Hey there," he said, in that lazy way that made a woman want to jump from the middle of the stairs right into his muscular arms. She decided she wasn't athletic enough - or brave enough - for a jump like that.

"Oh, hello."

"That was quite a show you were putting on. Sorry I missed the big finale."

She slowly walked down the stairs. "You really missed a spectacle. I was going to jump over to the chandelier, do a spin, and land right there where you're standing."

He smiled. "Well, then, it sounds like my life was in danger, and I didn't even know it."

She finally made it to the bottom of the stairs. "Do you come here often?"

Reed tilted his head slightly. "Was that a pickup line?"

Shelby laughed. "No. It's just that this is the second time I've run into you here, and now that I work here..."

He looked down at her name tag. "You work here now?"

"As of today."

"Congratulations on the new job!"

"Thanks. I was in real estate, but decided to do something a little different for a while."

"New beginnings are always a good thing."

"So, can I help you with anything?"

"Actually, yes. I'm looking for a book about social media marketing. I was going to hire someone, but I like to understand concepts before I delegate."

"Our business section is right over here," she said, leading him to the other side of the room. "I know these are about entrepreneurship, these are about marketing, and we have a few that are specific to social media."

He smiled. "You're already pretty good at your job."

"Thanks." She stood there silent for a moment. "Well, if you need anything else, just let me know."

He nodded and went back to looking at the books. Shelby slipped away out of sight so she could take a moment to mentally abuse herself for dancing like an idiot where anyone - especially Mr. Hot Stuff - could see her.

What was it about this particular man that made her sweat all over? She'd seen handsome men before, but he just had *something*. She couldn't put her finger on it. Well, she could, but she'd probably get arrested.

"I think I'll take this one," he said from behind her, causing her to jump.

"Okay, great," she said, hurrying toward the register.

"Did I scare you?"

"No, not at all," she said, not looking up and instead focusing on scanning the price sticker on his book.

"You jumped."

She sighed. "Okay, fine. You scared me. I was lost in thought, and I didn't expect you'd be done looking so fast."

"It's a tiny bookstore," he said, chuckling.

"That'll be twenty-one dollars and thirty-eight cents."

He reached for his wallet and pulled out his credit card. "Here you go."

"Thanks." She ran his credit card and printed the receipt, slipping it into a white paper bag with the Tattered Pages logo printed on it. She handed the bag to him. "Here you go. Hope it helps."

Reed took the bag and smiled. "Thanks." He turned and walked toward the door, but turned around. "I liked your dancing."

Shelby laughed. "Yeah, I bet you did."

One side of his mouth curved upward, revealing a lone dimple. "I'm not kidding. Maybe you can show me some of those moves sometime."

She stood there without speaking as Reed slipped out the door and down the sidewalk. What in the heck did that mean? Was he hinting at asking her out? Why did she suddenly feel like a teenager again, and was that even a good thing?

Cami stared at her computer screen. Today her plan was to contact her whole friends list on social media and explain her new business to them. Surely someone would want to join. She believed in the products, and she knew she could build a huge team if people would just listen without judgment. Getting people not to judge the things in her life had proven hard over the years.

As she stared at the screen, her phone rang from its charging perch on the desk, startling her. She quickly grabbed it and answered.

"Hello?" When she heard her husband's voice, everything in her body relaxed. It'd been so long since she'd heard from him, and she was extremely relieved.

"Hey, baby," he said, the same way he'd always said it. She missed him. His arms, his jaw stubble, his smell.

"I was so worried about you!" She unexpectedly burst into tears. Not having Dominic at home with her was so difficult.

"I know, and I'm sorry. You know it's not always possible for me to get to a phone."

"I know, but I just miss you so much." She laid her head on her desk, the phone on speaker next to her cheek.

"I miss you too. How's everything going there?"

"Working all the time, as you know. Trying to build this business, but nobody wants to hear about it. I got invited to a new book club."

"A book club? Where?"

"A new lady moved onto our street and started a book club."

There was a long pause. "You know you can't tell these women a bunch of stuff, Cami."

She sat up, aggravated. "I've kept your secrets for a long time, Dom. I'm not stupid. I know what to say."

"You know it's not about me. This is all for you too, Cam."

She wanted to believe that. She wanted to believe the best about the man she married, but things hadn't exactly gone as planned after the wedding. Her family had warned her against marrying a man who wouldn't be around much, who wouldn't be a real partner in her marriage, but sometimes love makes you do crazy things. Now her family was barely speaking to her, and she'd never felt more lonely in her life.

"Things could've been different, Dom. If you'd chosen another line of work, we'd be together right now. This being apart isn't what I signed up for when I walked down the aisle."

He sighed. "I know. Things got much more involved than I planned, baby. But we'll be together soon. I promise."

"Are you okay?" she asked softly.

"As okay as I can be without you."

The next few minutes were spent chatting about this and that, and then he had to go. He always had to go so quickly. There was never enough time.

After she hung up, she leaned back against the chair and looked at the ceiling. Why did her life feel like she was on a never-ending hamster wheel? This wasn't what she had planned when she was a little girl. Back then, she was convinced she'd be a super-model or a doctor who cured cancer. Now, she was a lonely married woman whose husband wasn't there. She had multiple jobs, plenty of bills, and nobody was asking her to be a supermodel.

CHAPTER 6

AFTER WORKING THREE DAYS STRAIGHT, SHELBY WAS happy to host book club tonight. Thankfully, the food was being provided by everybody else, and all she had to do was make sure her house was clean and tidy. So far, she'd heard from Willadeene, Joan, Lacy, Cami, and a woman named Daniela that she didn't really know that well. According to Lacy, she was Italian, beautiful, and impossibly rich. Shelby didn't know what that last part meant.

"Your house smells divine," Lacy said upon entering. Shelby had lit her favorite candle, Sweet Tea and Pound Cake. It sounded weird, but it smelled like heaven.

"It's making me hungry."

Lacy smiled. "Well, lucky you because I brought my famous chicken casserole, and some fresh baked macadamia nut cookies for dessert. Where can I put them?"

"Right there on the breakfast bar. Thank you."

Shelby continued welcoming her guests as they entered. Cami brought wine and crackers. Joan brought a fruit tray. Daniela brought pasta salad. So far, it was shaping up to be a very good dinner.

Everyone mingled for a few minutes, but when seven o'clock rolled around, Shelby got everyone's attention.

"So glad to have everyone here again tonight. I see we lost a few people."

Cami laughed. "They probably couldn't read."

"Well, at any rate, I thought we could chat about the book and then eat. Sound good?" Everyone nodded. "Okay, so on our group text, I said let's all read the first two chapters and discuss. Does anyone want to start?"

Lacy raised her hand and then spoke at the same time. "I have to say I'm not a fan of the heroine so far."

"Really? Why?" Cami asked.

"Well, she seems rather weak. I mean, her husband cheats, and she stays with him at first, letting him continue to live in her home and sleep in her bed."

"Maybe she forgives easily," Cami said.

"I agree with this one," Daniela said, pointing at

Lacy, her accent as thick as if she walked out of an Italian movie. "I would kill him."

Shelby laughed. "That's one way to handle it."

"I mean seriously, if a husband cheats, he has to pay. It's the way things should be," she said, her chin jutted out.

"I don't think everyone has to react the same way as you, Lacy," Cami said.

"So, if your husband cheated while he was away on one of his military excursions, you'd just welcome him home with open arms?"

"Not necessarily. I'm just saying that sometimes relationships are more complicated than they appear. Sometimes they're worth saving, and that takes work on both sides."

Lacy laughed under her breath. "Any strong woman would make him pay dearly."

"Okay, ladies, let's move on. Joan, what did you think of the first two chapters?" Shelby asked, noticing that Joan was being very quiet.

"Well, I think we shouldn't judge others unless we want to be judged."

"Oh, dear Lord," Lacy groaned. "Some people deserve judgment. And punishment."

Shelby got the distinct impression that someone had cheated on Lacy in the past. Maybe it was her husband, or maybe it was an old boyfriend. Shelby didn't know, and she sure as heck wasn't going to ask.

"On to chapter two. In this chapter, our heroine leaves her husband and takes a chance on herself. She moves to an island in the Caribbean and starts working at a resort. What did you think about this part, Cami?"

"I think I'd love to live on an island."

"Really? I'd be scared to start over like that out in the middle of the ocean," Joan said.

"No risk, no reward. Sometimes you just have to do things that nobody expects. It keeps life interesting," Lacy said. Shelby was learning a lot about these women already.

"What have you done to keep life interesting, Lacy?" Cami asked.

"That sounds like an accusatory question."

"No, not at all. It's just that by outward appearances, you seem like the world's perfect wife and mother. You bake cakes, volunteer at the PTA, organize the neighborhood watch. I just didn't peg you as the risk-taking type."

"Well, Cami, you don't know me very well then," she said, pasting on a smile.

"So, back to the original question. What do you do to keep life interesting?"

"It's hard to do a lot with small children, as you

may imagine, but I have my hobbies. I like to try all sorts of new things."

"Like new recipes?" Cami asked, obviously picking at her.

Lacy smiled again. "Yes, new recipes. That's just what I mean."

There was a long, awkward silence before Shelby picked the conversation back up again. "I just noticed Willadeene didn't make it here tonight. Has anyone seen her?"

"You mean the crazy lady?" Daniela asked, taking a long sip of her wine. "I haven't seen her in a couple of days."

Shelby had a bad feeling in her gut. "Should we go check on her?"

"Why? It's nice and calm over here. No need to bring in a troublemaker," Lacy said.

"She's just a lonely old woman," Joan interjected. "She'd probably appreciate someone checking on her."

Lacy groaned. "Fine. We'll walk over there…"

"Y'all better not have eaten without me!" They all turned and saw Willadeene walking through the front door, the normal scowl on her face.

"You're late, Willadeene," Cami said.

"Did you eat yet?"

"Not yet."

"Then I'm not late."

"The point of book club is to discuss the book," Shelby reminded her.

"Not for me, it isn't." She plopped down on the sofa next to Joan.

"Oh, really?" Lacy asked.

"Look, I'm an old lady who gets no visitors, so I never get to go out to eat. I eat those microwave meals. If I know a good meal is happening over here, I'm coming. But I ain't reading that book."

Shelby decided not to say anything else. "We're not quite done discussing the book, but we'll eat soon."

Willadeene rolled her eyes. "My blood sugar is getting low, so make it snappy."

"Going down our list of questions... here's a good one. Our heroine decides to renovate a place by herself, doing all the manual labor and everything. What's the hardest thing you've ever done in your life?"

Everyone sat quietly for a moment until Daniela spoke up. "Moving to the United States without speaking the language was difficult."

"That's a good one. I can't imagine how hard that was," Shelby said. She was always impressed at people who left everything they knew in another country and went somewhere they didn't even know the language.

"What did she say?" Willadeene asked, leaning

over to Joan and whispering not so softly. Shelby gave her a look.

"What about you Cami?"

"What I'm doing now is the hardest thing I've done. Being without my husband." Her eyes welled with tears. "Sorry. I spoke to him today, and it just made me miss him more."

"I'm so sorry, Cami. I can't relate, but I'm sure everyone here thanks you and your husband for your service."

"What kind of service?" Willadeene asked.

"Her husband is in the military and has been gone a long time," Shelby said. Willadeene's eyebrows furrowed together, but she said nothing else.

"Can we move to the next person?" Cami asked.

"Of course. What about you, Joan?"

"Losing my husband has been the hardest thing I've ever done. I miss him every single day, just like he passed yesterday." Her eyes welled with tears, too.

"Oh, dear Lord! I didn't know this was going to be a sob fest," Willadeene said, throwing her hands in the air.

"Willadeene! Have some compassion!" Shelby said. She was very close to throwing this woman out of her house.

"I have compassion, but I thought this was a fun book club. I've only got limited time left on this planet, and right now y'all are making me want to jump off the balcony out there."

There was a long silence before everyone, except Willadeene, started laughing. When they finally stopped laughing, Shelby looked at Lacy.

"Lacy, what's the hardest thing you've done?"

She shrugged her shoulders. "I don't really have one. I guess my life has been pretty blessed."

"You've never done anything hard? Seriously?" Cami said.

"Nope. Now, how about we go eat? I'm starving!" Lacy suddenly stood up and walked toward the kitchen. Cami looked at Shelby in confusion.

"Okay, well, uh… Yeah, let's eat, I guess. We'll focus on the next two chapters for next week, okay?"

Everyone agreed and then headed to the kitchen to eat. Shelby didn't know what book clubs were supposed to be like, but this one seemed awfully strange. For the first time, she was second guessing her decision to start one.

Shelby straightened books on the marketing shelf for the third time in the last hour. She was bored. Nobody came in during the midmorning hours, and it was driving her crazy. She liked to be busy, and this job was proving to be very different from real estate.

In her days as an agent, she woke up early and started driving the area looking for "for sale by owners". These were the people with for sale signs in their yards but weren't using real estate agents. She left flyers and sometimes called in an effort to get them to sign with her.

Then she'd follow up with clients, show properties, list houses, and manage her staff. It was an exhausting business, but a busy one. It kept her mind occupied, which was always a good thing. Adjusting to a quieter suburban life and working at a bookstore was harder than she'd imagined it would be.

The door opened, and she was surprised to see Joan standing there. "Hey, Joan!"

"Hi," she said in her normal soft voice.

"Can I help you with something?"

"I'm looking for a book about caring for an aging parent."

"Okay, we have some books over here about that. Do you need help choosing an assisted living or nursing home?"

"No. More about helping them understand they can't do it alone anymore."

Shelby smiled sadly. "Your parents?"

"My mother. She's getting forgetful, and I can't make her understand that it's time to get some help.

She's in her mid-eighties, but she thinks she's twenty-five."

Shelby couldn't help but laugh. Her mother was in her seventies and wouldn't settle down either. "Here's one about that subject. And here's another one about helping get finances and other important paperwork organized."

Joan took both books and looked at them. "You know, it's hard to watch your parents get older and start to fail. My father passed a couple of years ago after being in a nursing home for two years. He'd always been my hero. So big and strong. To watch his memories disappear to where he no longer recognized me was one of the worst things that's ever happened to me."

Shelby could feel the sadness in her voice. "I can only imagine. My mother is still well, but I worry about the day when she's not."

"My mother has been sick for a week now with some kind of chest cold. I'm going to stay with her for a few days. She lives on Pawley's Island, so not too terribly far."

Shelby had no idea where that was, but she'd look it up on the map later. "Can I do anything to help?"

"No, but thank you. If you see anybody at my house that shouldn't be there, can you let me know?"

"Of course."

"I think I'll get both of these. Never hurts to have plenty of information."

"Absolutely."

Shelby rang her up and waved goodbye as Joan left. There was something about her that bothered Shelby. The sadness and grief over losing her husband six years ago seemed to only be part of the puzzle. Shelby had no idea what the other part was, but she hoped Joan could live a happier life somehow.

As Joan walked back into her house, she felt a deep sense of dread. There was a part of her that wanted to be connected to her neighbors and have friends. Then there was the other part of her that knew she could never do that. Everything was just too far gone.

She walked into her kitchen and put the books she had bought on top of a stack of stuff. It seemed like she always had so many piles of stuff everywhere. She wanted to believe that everybody had this much clutter, but she knew that probably wasn't the case.

The thing was, she just didn't care anymore. She didn't care about keeping a clean house. She didn't care about much of anything. Every day was just a slow slog through her life.

And now, with her mother being sick, she feared she would lose the very last person who loved her. And she had been pretty hard to love.

Most people didn't understand her, which was why she didn't have a big circle of friends. Even her extended family members had long ago walked away from her. They didn't understand the way she'd grieved losing her husband, and they didn't understand her way of dealing with other things.

She walked into her living room and sat down in her favorite chair, putting her feet up on the ottoman. She really needed to clean up in here. Things were getting a little out of hand. She could barely see the TV now.

When they had moved to Waverly Lane all those years ago, Joan had had big plans. She always kept a very tidy house and enjoyed having friends and family over. When Andrew died, a huge part of her died. It was like her love and zest for life had been sucked straight out of her body. She had expected it to come back, for the grief to eventually fade. But it never did.

She had never dated again because no man could compare to the one she already had. Why settle for second best, she figured.

Joining the book club was the most courageous

thing that she had done since her husband died. She didn't even really know why she did it. It was risky, for sure. What if they wanted to have an event at her house? What if they wanted to be genuine friends and stop by with a basket of bread? What if there was some emergency and one of her neighbors needed to stay at her house for a day or two?

These were all things that she thought about before she walked into that first book club meeting. But there was a part of her that knew that she needed that interaction. She needed people in her life or else she just might die. If she lost her mother, who would she have then?

She had to make friends. She had to care about other people. Otherwise, what was the point of life?

As she switched on the television and turned on her favorite court TV show, she stared straight ahead, not really watching it. Somehow, she had to find a way to get back into life. As hard as it was, she thought it was still worth doing. A little glimmer of hope was supposed to be a good thing, but for her, it felt very dangerous.

If there was one thing that Shelby knew she needed for her mental health, it was exercise. Most of the time, she liked to take an early morning run, but her knee had been bothering her lately. She supposed that was the price of getting older.

When she woke up this morning, she made the rash decision to show up at Cami's yoga class. She'd tried yoga a couple of times before, each time failing miserably. It didn't matter how in shape she was, her flexibility was definitely lacking.

But she couldn't get out of it now. Cami had just seen her walk through the front door. When she saw all the petite soccer moms wearing their yoga pants and spandex shorts, she had second thoughts. Cami grabbed her arm and pulled her into the class before she could get away.

"I hope this is a beginner's class," Shelby said, looking around. Judging from the women she saw, this was definitely no beginner's class. They all looked taut and tight and perfect. Blonde hair, high ponytails and cute button noses. She felt like a giant donkey in front of them.

"Every yoga class is a beginner's class. We can tailor the class to your needs. Nobody is more advanced than somebody else. Yoga is available to everyone."

Shelby knew that sounded good in theory, but she was also a realist. There was a very good chance she was going to fall on her face or fracture her hip during this class.

Still, she found a spot, rolled out the mat Cami

gave her, and prayed. She just needed to get through this class, pump up her endorphins, and get on with her day. Thankfully, she had the day off, so she could get some things around the house done. There were so many little projects that were still outstanding since she moved in.

Cami began the class by having everyone close their eyes and take some deep breaths. She could hear other people filtering into the class, and she hoped some of them were like her. Newbies. Inflexible.

She felt somebody sit down next to her, roll out a mat, and sit down. Not wanting to open her eyes because of how she'd been taught in church as a kid, she continued taking her breaths in and out. It felt kind of good, actually. She enjoyed the relaxation.

A few moments later, they all opened their eyes, and Cami instructed them to sit cross-legged and raise one arm over their head and lean to the opposite side. When Shelby did this, she came face-to-face with the person sitting next to her.

Reed Sullivan.

Seriously? What kind of game was the universe trying to play on her? It was getting pretty ridiculous. She felt like somebody was following her around with hidden cameras, trying to see her reaction every time she made a fool of herself in front of this man.

"We meet again," he whispered, smiling. Dang dimple.

"I'm pretty sure you're following me." She wanted to follow that up with telling him she would call the police but he was too handsome so she couldn't bring herself to dial the number. She thought better of it.

"Nope. I've been coming to this class for a few weeks now. It helps me keep my stress levels down."

"Well, then I guess I need to be here because my stress levels are through the roof. Of course, that's nothing new. I like to maintain a really high stress level so as not to shock my body," she said, laughing. One of her worst habits was talking a lot and quickly when she got nervous.

"We'd better stop talking or the teacher might call us out," he said, winking. Oh Lord. He winked? Winking *and* dimples? A killer combination.

"Right."

The rest of the class was a whirlwind of twists and breaths and holds, but Shelby didn't care because every few minutes, Reed Sullivan would smile at her in a way that gave her shivers in places she didn't know she had. She knew he wasn't the least bit interested in her. He could have his pick of the women in Charleston and beyond. Plus, he'd made it clear that he *wasn't* asking her on a date when he invited her to his restaurant. Still, a woman was allowed to have illogical crushes on hot restauranteurs.

"Excellent class," he said at the end, wiping his forehead with a small hand towel he'd brought. She remembered when Roger would work out and sweat everywhere. It grossed her out, so she asked him to wipe his forehead. He'd told her it was manly to sweat and get over it.

"It was. I didn't know I even had some of those muscles."

He laughed. "You'll get the hang of it."

"Oh no, I won't be back. I don't think I'm very good at yoga," she said, rolling up her mat and standing up.

"You only get good by practicing. Listen, I used to be on a blood pressure medicine because of stress. I was able to go off of it by doing yoga and eating a little healthier."

"Really? Maybe I should try it again. I just don't think I'm very good at it."

"I think you did great," he said, smiling again. "Do you like Cuban sandwiches?"

"I love them. Why?"

"I make a great Cuban. You should come eat one."

She wasn't falling for this again. "I'll grab one the next time I place a to-go order."

He tilted his head slightly. "A to-go order? Are

you saying you don't want to sit across the table from me and eat a sandwich, Shelby?"

Her eyes widened. "Oh… wait… are you asking me…"

Reed laughed. "Sorry. I know we got our wires crossed the first time. I am, in fact, asking you to go with me to eat lunch right now."

"But I'm a sweaty mess." What was it about her that she had to sweat profusely every time this man was around?

He leaned closer, like he was going to tell her a secret. "So am I. And guess what? I own the restaurant, so I can look as bad as I want and still get a table."

"Well, I am hungry," she said, acting like it was a big decision. It wasn't.

"Great. I'll go bring my car around. It's the black BMW."

"Sounds good." She watched him walk out and then started internally freaking out. She hadn't been on a date of any kind, even a simple lunch, in well over ten years. Was this really a date? Instead of asking herself more questions she couldn't answer, Shelby ran to the bathroom and wiped as much sweat off as she could.

CHAPTER 7

SHELBY SAT ACROSS FROM REED AND THOUGHT ABOUT how much better looking he was than Roger. Reed had that distinguished look about him, and most men didn't have that.

Her grandmother would've described how she felt about Reed as smitten. She was definitely feeling smitten at the moment. When he'd picked her up in front of the yoga studio, he had gotten out and opened her door. It was one of those southern gentlemen things she'd always dreamed of, and she'd felt butterflies zipping around in her stomach.

Then they had pulled up at his restaurant, which was not even open for lunch yet. Reed unlocked the door and told his kitchen staff what they wanted to order. They had the restaurant all to themselves for another twenty minutes before the doors opened for lunch.

"Well, what do you think?"

"I think this is the best Cuban sandwich I've ever had in my life."

He beamed. "That's what I wanted to hear. What about the salad? Do you like the dressing?"

She chewed and swallowed. "Yes, I love it. What is this again?"

"It's a raspberry and fig vinaigrette I've been experimenting with lately."

"You're very talented, Reed. I mean, to not only come up with the recipes, but to run such a successful restaurant."

"I have lots of help, trust me. How are you liking the bookstore?"

She chuckled. "It's a lot slower pace than I'm used to, but I'm enjoying it. I love to read, so being surrounded by books is always a good thing to me."

"Yeah, I love to read as well. Of course, I'm always too busy to do it, but when I can, I enjoy it."

"When is the last time you read for enjoyment?"

He thought for a moment. "Maybe three years ago? I won a trip to St. Thomas and got to go away for four glorious days. I literally laid on the beach and read most of the time."

"Three years ago? I see now why you're trying to reduce stress. You need more time off for yourself."

He took a sip of his sweet tea. "I'm with myself a lot. I don't need more time with the thoughts in here," he said, pointing at his head.

"I know what you mean. I've been alone a lot lately, and I was starting to miss other people's company. I guess that's why I formed the book club."

"I just work so much. I'm around a lot of people all day and night, but I don't really have a social life, if that makes sense. My work is my social life."

"And do you like it that way?"

He shrugged his shoulders. "I thought I did. When I was younger and working my way up the career ladder, it wasn't so bad. I dated here and there, had some friends. But when you hit a certain level of work ethic, people start to fall away. The next thing I knew, I was in my forties with no wife or kids. And then the gossip starts."

"Gossip?" she said, acting as if she didn't know people would talk about a man in his forties who'd never been married.

"Apparently, if you're a man in your forties who has never married, you're gay or some kind of serial killer."

Shelby laughed. "Well, are you either of those things?"

"No."

"Sorry, I didn't mean to make light of it."

"You're divorced, right?"

"Yep. Recently."

"Sorry."

She waved her hand at him and took a bite of her food. "It's no biggie."

Reed stared at her. "No biggie?"

Realizing how she sounded, she put down her fork. "Wow, that probably seemed like I was making light of divorce, and I'm not."

"Sounds like there's a story in there somewhere," he said, pinching off a piece of bread and popping it into his mouth.

"The short version is that I got married to a man I didn't really love in the way you should love your husband. We were much more business partners than life partners. As you can imagine, that didn't work so well."

"And you've just touched on the reason I've never been married."

"What do you mean?"

"It's not because I enjoy dating, and it's not because I hate marriage. It's because I love my business, and I just haven't felt the same kind of love for a person. Is that weird?"

"I don't think so. You just haven't found your person yet."

"And I guess you haven't found yours either."

"My grandma used to say there's a lid for every pot. I'm not sure I buy it. Maybe some people aren't meant to be in love."

"That would be really sad, I would think."

"Well, all I can say is that I've been in a long-term relationship that wasn't true love, and I'd much rather be alone forever than go through that again."

There was a momentary pause in the conversation before Reed chuckled. "This is kind of heavy for lunch conversation."

Shelby laughed. "Maybe we need some wine."

By the time Shelby made it home from yoga and her lunch with Reed, she was exhausted yet walking on cloud nine. Reed was engaging and fun and smart. Had she met a man like him before Roger, her life would've been different.

Whether or not it was a date, she still didn't know, but she did know she had a great time. There was no fighting. No awkward pauses. Just great conversation and lots of laughs.

Shelby pulled into her driveway and stepped out into the hot Charleston sun. Her plan was to take a quick shower and start sorting through the last of her kitchen boxes. How had she accumulated so many gadgets? When was the last time she made zucchini noodles, anyway?

Just as she was closing her car door, she glanced

across the street at Joan's house. She could see water leaking out of Joan's side porch area. She knew Joan was out of town visiting her sick mother, so it made no sense that water would even be on, much less flowing over the steps of her porch.

Without thinking, Shelby ran across the street and peeked into the porch area. There were some boxes stacked in there, and she worried the water would damage whatever was inside.

"Everything okay?" Cami called from the end of the driveway after apparently having seen Shelby sprint across the road.

"Her whole enclosed porch is filling with water. We've got to get this door open and see what's going on. She's out of town," Shelby called back.

Cami ran closer. "Oh, my gosh! What on earth? Here, let's try to pry the door open." She pulled a pocketknife out of her purse. Shelby gave her a strange look. "What? My grandpa taught me to always carry a knife. Comes in handy, like right now."

Cami fiddled with the lock on the door, and it finally popped open. "What's going on?"

They turned to see Lacy standing there. "Joan is out of town, and water is leaking out of her house," Shelby said as they finally pulled open the door.

Shelby and Cami walked up the three steps and pushed open the porch door. When Shelby got inside, she was shocked at what she saw. There were boxes everywhere, as if Joan had just moved in or was moving out.

"What is all this?" Cami asked.

"No idea. They're almost up to the ceiling."

"Where's the water coming from?"

They walked over to the glass door leading into the house. "It's locked," Shelby said after trying the handle.

"Let me do it," Lacy said, walking in behind them. She pulled out a credit card and quickly popped open the door. Shelby and Cami stared at her. "What? So I can break into houses easily. It's a talent, not a crime, ladies."

"I'm actually impressed," Cami said.

"You would be," Lacy shot back. The two women seemed to take great pride in picking on each other.

Shelby entered the house and ran straight to the kitchen sink, which was on. Somehow Joan must've turned on the water to fill up the sink and forgot about it. The last time Shelby had talked to her, she was a bit distracted and possibly depressed.

"What in the world?" Lacy said, her hand over her mouth. Shelby had been so focused on the sink that she hadn't seen anything else.

"I've never seen anything like this," Cami said.

Shelby looked in their direction and was dumbfounded. The kitchen was mainly clean, but when she looked into what must've been the living room, it was stacked floor to ceiling with boxes of all different sizes.

"What is all this crap?" Lacy asked.

"Maybe she sells something? Like, is this inventory?" Cami asked, walking closer to the living room.

"I don't think so," Shelby said. "I think she's a hoarder."

"A hoarder? Certainly not. That doesn't happen in this neighborhood," Lacy said, shaking her head.

"Hoarding is a mental condition, Lacy. That doesn't discriminate based on neighborhood," Cami said. "This is so very sad."

"How could this be happening so close and nobody knew?" Lacy asked.

"Until the book club, none of you knew each other. She's been over here struggling alone."

"I feel awful now," Cami said.

"Let's get some towels and clean up this water before it ruins her floors."

For the next few minutes, Shelby and Cami did their best to sop up the water. Lacy had a wet/dry vacuum at her house that she also brought over. Thankfully, they were able to get the water cleaned up in about half an hour.

"We should probably get out of here. We're really violating her privacy," Shelby said. They walked outside and stood in the driveway.

"I wonder what the rest of the house looks like," Lacy said, scrunching her nose.

"Hey, don't be judgy. Everybody has secrets they don't want other people to see," Cami said.

"I don't," Lacy responded.

"Well, either way, we have to help her. She can't keep living like that. It's awful. There's no way she could get out of there in the event of a fire," Shelby said, looking back at the house. It was so beautiful on the outside, yet such a mess on the inside. The metaphor really hit her. So many people looked great on the outside, but were a mess on the inside, too.

"How can we help her?" Lacy asked.

Shelby thought for a moment. "What about an intervention?"

"An intervention? Like for alcoholics and drug addicts?"

"Lacy, you can do interventions for other things," Cami said, rolling her eyes. "I think it's a good idea. When does she get home?"

"I'm not sure. Her mother is sick. Hopefully a few days?"

"Okay. When we see her come home, we'll ask if she can come to your house," Cami said. "Then we can talk to her. She'll know she has friends, people who care."

"It depends on what day. I have tennis lessons

and a nail appointment this week," Lacy said, looking down at her nails. The women stared at her. "What? I need nice nails. It's a self-care thing."

"Can we agree on one thing?" Cami asked.

"What?" Shelby said.

"Nobody tells Willadeene. It'll be all over the neighborhood."

"Forget the neighborhood. If Willadeene finds out, it'll be on the local news," Lacy said, causing Cami to laugh. Maybe there was hope for those two after all.

"Okay, we keep this to ourselves. It's nobody's business anyway," Shelby said. They all nodded and then said goodbye, walking to their own homes.

Lacy sat at her computer in her hobby room, staring at the blinking cursor. She often did this, allowing her mind to wander instead of doing the thing she did best.

Actually, she was probably a better mother than anything. She adored her children in a way that she couldn't have described before having them. It was that protection of them that made her do the things she did. It was her overwhelming need to take care of them that caused her to make certain choices that other people probably wouldn't make.

She looked out the window at Shelby's house just down the street. What a blessing she had been given to be able to start her life over. To wipe the slate clean and paint on a canvas exactly what she wanted her life to be.

It wasn't so easy for Lacy. Having children caused her to have complications other people might not have had. She wouldn't let them live the life she had as a child. She would do everything she could to make their lives appear to be perfect. She wanted them to think she got up early every day just to hang the sun in the sky for them.

When she walked into Joan's house and saw the hoarding situation, it made her sad. She almost became nauseous. But Lacy wasn't one to show her cards. She wasn't the type of person who got into deep, emotional conversations.

As much as she wished she were different, Lacy was a very "surface level" kind of person. She didn't want people knowing her problems. She didn't want to talk about her feelings. But the more she hung out with the women in her neighborhood, the more she felt like confiding in one of them, and that was a dangerous thing.

She had built her life like a house of cards. If one slipped away, the whole thing was going to fall. She just couldn't risk that.

Oh, how people would sit in judgment of her if

they really knew what was going on. She couldn't have that. The reputation of her family meant a lot to her.

She stood up and walked out of her hobby room and down the stairs to get herself a glass of water. To her surprise, Ed was standing in the kitchen, leaning against the counter.

"What are you doing here? You should be at work."

"My meeting ended early, so I thought I'd come home for a while."

"Ed, you know our agreement."

He looked at her for a moment, obviously trying to choose his words wisely. Lacy wasn't a person he wanted to argue with. She almost always won even though he was the attorney.

"This is my house too, Lacy."

"That may very well be true, but we made a decision about how we were going to handle things a long time ago. I can't just be walking downstairs and finding you standing in the kitchen without warning."

He threw his hands in the air. "Dang it, Lacy. We were supposed to iron all of this out. I don't like the way things are going. This will not work long-term."

"You don't get to decide about this! I will not have my children growing up·in a home where their parents hate each other."

A few moments later, Nicolai started crying in the other room.

"I'm going to go get my son," Ed said, walking past her. Lacy slapped her palm against the center of his chest, pushing him back slightly.

"One time, Ed. One time. You made an agreement. At least try to keep this one. Don't show up like this again without contacting me. You know what I'll do if you don't keep your word."

He sucked in a breath and blew it out, his nostrils flaring. "This isn't what I wanted, Lacy."

She laughed under her breath. "Well, I guess you should've thought about that, huh?"

He stared straight ahead and waited for her to remove her hand before he continued up the stairs toward the nursery. Lacy stood at the edge of her immaculate kitchen and then straightened her shirt.

"Today is a good day to have a good day," she said to herself before walking upstairs.

When the time for the next book club rolled around, Shelby felt edgy. Joan had just arrived back at her home earlier in the day, so they hadn't had a chance to plan an intervention.

"Should we do it tonight?" Cami asked, standing

in Shelby's kitchen. She finished tossing the salad and set it in the refrigerator.

"I don't think so. Wouldn't that be an ambush?"

Cami laughed. "Isn't that what an intervention is, anyway? You're not supposed to let the person know what's coming, right?"

"Yeah, but everyone will be here. It's not fair to air her dirty laundry in public."

"Dirty laundry in the most literal sense of the word," Lacy said from the breakfast bar where she was busy frosting a cake she'd brought.

"I say we ask her to stay afterward with just the three of us. We'll sit her down, tell her what happened, and let her know she has our support," Cami said.

Shelby nodded. "Okay. But what if she doesn't come? I mean, she just got home from an emotional visit with her mother. Maybe she's too tired and will stay home to relax."

"How could a person relax in that house?" Lacy asked.

"I have no idea."

Book club was going to start in about twenty minutes, so the women set all the food up on the kitchen table and walked out into the living room.

Soon after, people started knocking on the front door, including Willadeene, who was never late. She had learned her lesson that if she didn't sit through

the part where they talked about the book, she
would not get the food.

Shelby wondered if Willadeene had enough food
in her house. Maybe she was struggling with
finances or something, but the woman sure loved
to eat.

Thankfully, Joan arrived for book club shortly
before they were to get started. Shelby made her way
over to speak to her.

"I'm so glad to see you. How is your mother?"

Joan looked down, her face sad. "Not good. I had
to hire a full-time caregiver to take care of her when
I'm not there. I'm planning to go back in a week
or so."

"I'm so sorry. I know that has to be hard."

"I wasn't going to come tonight. Honestly, I'm
exhausted, but I just didn't want to stay home."

Now Shelby knew why. Who would want to stay
in that house when they needed to get rest?

"Listen, Lacy, Cami and I are going to stay after
book club and have a cup of coffee. We'd love if
you'd join us."

Joan thought for a moment. "You know what? I'd
like that."

Shelby gathered everyone into the living room
and started the meeting. Willadeene, as per usual, sat
with a scowl on her face, waiting for the food part of
the evening to start.

"Thanks for coming, everyone. So, we read chapters three and four this week. What did everyone think?"

"I'm starting to really like our heroine. I feel like deciding to start over by herself took real courage," Cami said.

"See, I had a whole different take on that," Lacy said. "I feel like she could've fought harder to save her marriage. They had kids together."

Cami stared at her. "He cheated on her and got another woman pregnant. You don't think that's reason enough to leave?"

"Not necessarily. There are other options to make sure the children are happy."

"Wow. You must be a more forgiving woman than I am. Just the cheating would've sent me straight to his closet."

"His closet?"

"Yeah. His clothes would've been on the lawn or in a burn pile!"

The other women laughed, including Willadeene.

"I agree with Cami. If my husband had cheated, I'd have knocked him in the head with a shovel," Willadeene said loudly.

Nobody laughed, probably because they knew Willadeene would still knock someone in the head with a shovel if they crossed her.

"I think marriage is for life. My parents split

when I was young, and it forever altered who I was," Lacy said, sounding more sincere than Shelby had ever heard.

"Divorce is awful. My parents also divorced when I was a kid," Cami said.

"Well, sometimes people staying together for the kids is the worst thing they can do," Willadeene suddenly piped in.

"How so?" Lacy asked, seeming honestly curious.

"Back when I was a kid, people didn't get divorced so easily, and women didn't have the opportunities they do now. My dad was a horrible man, verbally abusive to us and my mother. When I turned ten years old, I begged her to leave him. She told me she couldn't do that. She said marriage was forever, and she said we had nowhere else to go, anyway."

The room was silent. "I'm so sorry to hear that, Willadeene. It sounds like you had a tough childhood."

She smiled slightly, looked off into space. "Not all the time. My mom made everything better. She spent time with us, taught us to cook and sew. My sister and I never wanted for anything, even though we barely had two nickels to rub together. She took all the abuse from our father, but it ruined her life."

"What do you mean?" Lacy asked.

"He got sick when I was eighteen, and she spent

the next ten years taking care of that old jerk. My sister and I left to get married. By the time he died, my mom got sick from the exhaustion. Her whole life was ruined by taking care of someone who never deserved a minute of her time, and we were miserable when he was around. So, sometimes staying together for the children is just an excuse."

Lacy shifted in her seat. "An excuse?"

"Yeah. Some people use it as an excuse to stay in a bad situation because they're too scared of what's on the other side of freedom."

Shelby couldn't help but agree with her. "That's how I feel too."

"Really, Shelby? You don't think marriage should be protected at all costs?" Lacy asked, her eyes wide.

"At all costs? No. I married a man I thought I loved. As the years went by, we both realized that we loved our business, but not each other. And then he found someone else. I wasn't even mad about it. I was relieved."

"Because it gave you an out?" Lacy asked.

"Partly. But also because of what Willadeene just said. I found myself no longer scared of what was on the other side. Now I just feel free."

"And lonely?"

She smiled at Lacy. "I'd rather be lonely sometimes than miserable all the time." Shelby didn't mean for it to come out condescending, but she knew it probably did.

After a pause in the conversation, "Well, I'm very thankful for a strong, happy marriage," Lacy said, smiling.

The rest of book club was boring in comparison, with lots of small talk about the characters and locations in the book. Shelby was glad when it was over and they could eat because she felt like there was a lingering tension in the air between her, Cami, and Lacy. The intervention with Joan was getting closer, and she had no idea what they were even going to say.

CHAPTER 8

SHELBY WAS STARTING TO SECOND GUESS THE WHOLE intervention idea. What she really wanted to do after eating so much food and dessert was take a hot bath and go to sleep. Instead, she was about to confront a neighbor she barely knew about her hoarding problem.

She cared about Joan, even though they had just met recently, but she didn't know how the woman was going to react. None of them knew her very well, and even though she seemed to be pretty mild-mannered, that didn't mean she wouldn't get irate when she heard they had been in her house. For all Shelby knew, she would call the police or something.

"Are you sure we should do this?" she asked Cami quietly in the corner of the kitchen.

Cami stared at her. "Do you really think the three

of us can keep this a secret? We can just go on living our lives like the woman is not living in her house with a ton of trash and boxes?"

Shelby shook her head. "No. We can't do that."

"Are you whispering about me?" Lacy asked, walking around the corner.

"No, we just say things to your face," Cami said, laughing.

"You're a real comedian."

"Where is Joan?"

"She went to the restroom."

"How do we start this?" Shelby asked.

"We just sit down and tell her. No beating around the bush."

"Oh, just as simple as that?" Lacy said, sarcastically.

"Am I interrupting?" Joan asked, unexpectedly walking into the kitchen.

"No, of course not," Shelby said, waving her hand. "I was just trying to decide if I should make regular coffee or decaf. It's getting kind of late. Do you have a preference?"

Joan shrugged her shoulders. "I don't have anything going on tomorrow, so regular is fine with me."

"Let me get that started. If you ladies want to just take a seat in the living room, I'll be out there in a minute."

The three of them walked into the living room and Shelby filled up the carafe with water, pouring it into the coffee machine. She didn't have one of those fancy coffee pots everybody else seemed to have. She used a good old-fashioned one like her mother and her grandmother before her.

A few moments later, she joined them in the living room. "The coffee is brewing."

Shelby sat down next to Cami on the love seat. Lacy sat on one end of the sofa and Joan on the other.

"I'm glad to get to stay after with you ladies. Not that I don't enjoy the other women in the club."

"Willadeene can be a bit much," Lacy said, rolling her eyes. The irony of that statement was that Lacy didn't realize that she too could be too much.

"She's different, that's for sure. Reminds me of my grandmother. She was kind of rough around the edges like that."

"Joan, we sort of wanted to talk to you about something," Shelby said, finally working up her nerve.

Joan tilted her head slightly. "Okay. What is it?"

"Well, while you were out of town, there was sort of a mishap."

"A mishap?"

"I was coming home one day, and I got out of my

car and just happened to notice that water was pouring out of your side porch."

"Water? That's weird. I wonder what was going on?"

"I saw Shelby walk across the street to take a closer look, so I joined her," Cami said, taking some of the load off Shelby.

"So what happened?"

"Well, I didn't want things to get ruined in your house, so Lacy and Cami helped me get the door open to your porch."

"You went onto my porch?"

"I did. And I know that's basically breaking and entering, but I was trying to save your property. That's when I noticed the water was also pouring out from under the door to your house."

"Why didn't you call someone instead of going inside?" Joan asked, obviously getting defensive. "Like the police or fire department? I mean, that's who you call in an emergency situation."

"There was no time. I didn't know what was happening inside, and I just wanted to get the water turned off. So we entered your home."

Joan sat there, her face turning redder and redder as she stared straight ahead, just past Shelby's right ear. She wouldn't look anybody in the eye.

"So you know?"

"We know," Lacy said, finally saying something.

"And I suppose you have decided to judge me. Bring out all of my dirty laundry right here?"

"That's not what we're trying to do, Joan. We care about you, and we want to help," Shelby said.

"Help? Who says I need help?" she said, almost laughing.

"Dear, it's obvious that you need help. Who would want to live like that?" Lacy said in her normal judgmental tone.

"Lacy!" Cami chided.

"I can't believe this!" Joan said, standing up.

"Joan, I was just trying to help. You forgot to turn off your kitchen sink somehow. I know you've been very distracted because of your mother."

"You should've called me. You have my phone number!"

"And what would you have said? Don't turn off my water? Let my floor cave in?" Cami asked, getting slightly irritated.

"I don't know what I would've said, but you didn't even give me the choice! I'm going home. I guess I'll lock my doors a little tighter from now on!"

Without another word, Joan walked out the front door and slammed it behind her. Shelby sat on her sofa in shock. Mild-mannered, quiet Joan didn't seem like the type the storm off and slam a door.

"Well, that didn't go like I had thought," Shelby said, looking at Cami.

"No, I didn't think it would go that way either."

"I'm going home. I've had about all the drama I can take for one night," Lacy said, standing up. "Do me a favor. If you ever think to have an intervention for me about something, just don't."

As Lacy walked out the door, Shelby sat there wondering what kind of crazy street she'd moved to. Just under the surface, she felt there were so many secrets out there. She was afraid Joan was just the tip of the iceberg.

Shelby was still a bit shaken after last night's book club and subsequent intervention with Joan.

As she tried to focus on her work at the bookstore, she couldn't help but think about how Joan felt today. Did she feel ganged up on? Did she feel judged?

Shelby didn't want her to feel either way. They just cared about her and wanted her to have a clean home.

Shelby had never really dealt with somebody who had a hoarding issue. She'd seen TV shows about it, but she had never understood it. Why would someone want to surround themselves with a bunch of stuff and trash? And in such a beautiful home?

She knew Joan was struggling with the grief of losing her husband six years ago, but a small part of her wondered why she couldn't move on? You can love someone, grieve their loss, and still move on with your life.

As she restocked the shelves in the gardening section, she also wondered about Joan's family. Surely she had brothers or sisters or cousins? Where were these people? Why weren't they in her life?

Shelby had always been interested in these kinds of questions. It wasn't that she loved gossip, per se, but that she enjoyed hearing the stories of other people's lives. She enjoyed learning about their relationships, their pasts, their quirks.

There were times she had even thought about becoming a fiction author herself, although she didn't think she had the talent for that. She wasn't sure exactly what her future held in the way of a career, but it didn't likely include publishing books.

She finished putting the last of the books up on the shelf and walked back to the front. The door opened just as she walked behind the counter, and Reed appeared.

"Hey there!" he said, smiling.

"Hey. What's going on?"

He pulled his hand from behind his back and held up a brown paper bag. "We had some leftovers at the restaurant during the lunch rush. I thought you might want something."

"Oh, yeah?" she said, smiling. She felt like a teenager again, with her high school crush giving her a Valentine's Day card.

"It's not much. A chicken Caesar salad. Do you like those?"

"I love those!" She reached her hand out and took the bag, looking inside. "What is this wrapped up?"

"Oh, that's a piece of our banana bread. Our pastry chef is amazing."

"I love banana bread too. Thank you for thinking of me."

He paused for a moment and then smiled. "If I'm being honest, you're pretty much all I've been thinking about since we had lunch the other day."

Shelby froze in place, unsure of what to say. It had been a very long time since any man had said something like that to her. Roger never said those sorts of things once they got out of the dating phase.

"Really?"

"Yes. And that's the other ulterior motive I had for coming here. I was wondering if you would go out on an official date with me, Shelby?"

"An official date? What does that include exactly?"

"Dinner, obviously. And then some sort of

activity seems warranted. Rollerskating? Miniature golf?"

She laughed. "That doesn't sound like something you would enjoy."

"I'm not as fancy as you think I am. Although if you take me rollerskating, I'll probably just break my tailbone."

"How about a movie?"

He nodded. "That sounds safer. Maybe we can leave the rollerskating for another time."

"Why don't we start with miniature golf, then bowling, and then we can try rollerskating?" she said, chuckling.

"That insinuates that we're going to have multiple dates. This is getting very serious."

Shelby stared at him for a moment. "I didn't mean…"

Reed laughed loudly. "I was joking, Shelby! Of course, I think we're going to have multiple dates. I mean, unless you turn out to be some kind of psycho. If you stand up on the dinner table at the restaurant and take off all your clothes, I'll probably look, but I might not ask for a second date."

Shelby didn't know that he had such a good sense of humor. She liked that. Roger had the sense of humor of a sleeping gnat.

"I will try to refrain from stripping naked in a restaurant. Are we going to your restaurant?"

"Of course not! That would be so tacky for me to take you to my own restaurant. I wouldn't have to spend any money."

"I wouldn't mind, Reed. I like your restaurant."

"Do you like French food?"

"Who doesn't?"

"There's a great French restaurant right in the heart of the French quarter. How about that?"

"That sounds amazing. When?"

"How about tomorrow night? I'll pick you up at six o'clock?"

Shelby grabbed a piece of paper and wrote down her address. She slid it across the counter toward him. "Sounds good. Here's my home address. Don't stalk me."

Reed looked down at it and smiled. "I'll try, but I can't promise anything."

As he waved and walked out the door, she put her elbows on the counter and her chin in her hands. If anybody was looking at her, she probably had little hearts floating above her head like in a cartoon. Shelby was definitely smitten with Reed Sullivan. Who wouldn't be? She didn't know how serious this would get, or if this would be their only date, but she was going to enjoy it no matter what.

Most days at the bookstore were fairly easy. Shelby was getting used to a slower pace of life outside of her field of real estate. She was still thinking about hanging her license with a local broker just so she could do some side business if she wanted to, but she didn't plan to go back to it as a full-time career, at least for the moment.

Today had been busier than normal at the bookstore, however, so she was looking forward to making a simple dinner and chilling out on the sofa until it was time to go to bed.

Just as she was putting on a pot of coffee and changing into her comfy clothes, she heard somebody ring the doorbell. For a moment, she hoped it was Reed. Maybe he had taken her address that she had written down for him, put it in his GPS, and arrived at her doorstep ready to whisk her out on a romantic date.

Of course, they had already set a date, but a girl could dream.

She opened the door to find Joan standing there, her face very serious. Shelby said nothing, but instead just looked at her.

"Do you mind if I come in?" Joan asked, her voice soft.

"Sure." Shelby stepped back and opened the door, allowing her inside. Joan walked into the living room where they had book club and sat down on the sofa, her hands in her lap.

"I'm surprised to see you here," Shelby said, sitting across from her on the loveseat.

"I know I'm probably not welcome in your house after screaming at you and then slamming your door like a toddler having a tantrum."

Shelby smiled slightly. "No, I totally understand why you got so upset. I'm sure you felt like we were ganging up on you, and like we invaded your privacy. We might have handled it the wrong way, but we were coming from a place of caring about you."

"I guess that was hard for me to believe at first. You ladies barely know me, so it just seemed like maybe I was being judged."

"I know, and I'm sorry. In my excitement of getting to know everybody here, I'm probably going to make some mistakes. I really just wanted to see what we can do to help you, Joan."

She sighed. "My life is overwhelming. I don't know that anybody can help me."

"Do you want to talk about it?"

"I don't know. I wouldn't want you to think less of me, although you've already seen the inside of my house, so I'm not sure how much less you can think of me."

"We don't think less of you. Everybody has challenges. We just want to help."

"I don't think Lacy really wants to help," Joan said, laughing.

"Well, we will just ignore her."

"When my husband died six years ago, we had a business together. We thrifted and sourced antiques, and we had a little store. Before he died, the store failed, so we had to move some of the inventory into the house. It wasn't as bad as it is now."

"What happened?"

"I think after he died, the only way I really felt close to him was when I was out shopping. That was our couple time. It was what we did for fun. Other people go on dates, and we went thrifting. It was great because we sold most of the stuff we got. But when I was doing it on my own and we didn't have a shop anymore, I just started bringing it into the house. And the garage. And the attic."

"That makes sense. Everybody deals with grief differently."

"It got out of hand, and then my son came for a surprise visit about three years ago. This is the house he last saw his dad in, and thought of it as his home. He was livid with me about how I had let things go. Not only had I filled it with crap, but I had stopped taking care of maintenance."

"So you haven't spoken to him since then?"

"I've tried. I send birthday cards and Christmas presents for him and his wife. He never responds. He told me that until I get my life together, he can't let me be in his."

That struck Shelby as so odd. Instead of trying to help his mother get through this difficult time in her life, it seemed her son had just abandoned her.

"I also lied about how my husband died. He wasn't in a work accident. He was an alcoholic and drank himself to death. I just didn't want anyone to think less of him because he was an amazing, loving husband."

"People can be amazing and still have their share of problems. How can we help you?"

"I don't really know. I just can't believe I let it get so out of hand. When y'all found out, I was just so deeply embarrassed that I couldn't face you, so I ran out. I blamed it on you, but it's my fault."

Shelby walked over and sat down next to Joan, squeezing her hand. "It's not your fault. You went through a very hard time in your life, and you didn't have any support. Now you do."

Joan smiled slightly. "I'm thankful you moved into the neighborhood, Shelby. And I'm sorry about how I acted."

"No need to apologize. Just think about how you want to move forward. If you want us to help you clean out the house, we'll do it. We can have a huge yard sale and help you raise the money you need to do maintenance on your house."

"I'll give it some thought. Just coming to talk to you was a big enough leap for today," she said, smiling sadly as she stood up.

Shelby walked her to the door. "You have people who care about you, whether or not you believe it," Shelby said, putting her hand on Joan's back.

"You know, I've lived here for many years, and until you came to town, I didn't know much of anyone on this street. Somehow, you've pulled a group of strangers together, and I appreciate that. I've felt so lonely since Andrew died."

"I'm glad I could help," Shelby said. With that, Joan walked down the front steps and down the driveway toward her house.

CHAPTER 9

SHELBY SAT ACROSS FROM REED, TRYING NOT TO STARE at him. He had the most amazing blue eyes, like two little pools of swirling Caribbean ocean water. She'd never seen someone with eyes quite like that, which was probably why he had women from three states chasing him.

The evening had started with Reed picking her up at her house and bringing her a bouquet of roses. She tried to remember a time Roger had done that, and she thought there was one Valentine's Day early in their relationship where he'd brought her fresh flowers from the grocery store. That was about the extent of his flower bringing.

As they drove to the restaurant, the conversation was pleasant and flowed well. She felt like she'd known Reed for a long time because everything was so easy. She felt comfortable with him, even though every time he looked at her, she felt a flurry of butterflies in her stomach.

Even though there was some small talk, it wasn't boring or monotonous. Shelby learned a lot about Reed's upbringing, his education, and his plans for the restaurant. She talked a lot about her family, where she grew up, and her inability to choose a new career path.

"So, you said you're going to hang your real estate license with a broker here?"

"Maybe. I mean, I'd like the opportunity to sell property if something comes up. I just don't want to do it as my day-to-day job anymore. I loved it for a long time, but I think it's inextricably connected to my ex-husband. Looking back, I don't know if I loved my job, or it was the only part of our relationship that was good. I just want to take some time to figure it out, and that can't be rushed."

"I firmly believe that everybody should find their dream job and go for it."

"Yeah, but some people don't have that opportunity. Everybody grows up in different situations, and some people never even see the possibilities."

"Well, for what it's worth, I hope you find what you love, Shelby. I know you enjoy the bookstore, but I think you're meant for even bigger things."

She smiled. "You think so?"

"Yes. You're smart, and I know you're a hard worker. Those are two of the most important things when it comes to building a business."

"Very true. Now enough of this talk about careers and business. I have an important question for you."

He put down his fork, folded his hands in front of him and stared at her with those icy blue eyes. "Okay, shoot."

"Did we miss the movie?"

His eyes widened, and he looked down at his watch. "Oh, my gosh! I'm so sorry, Shelby. I completely lost track of time."

She laughed. "I think it's actually a good thing."

"A good thing?"

"Well, it just means that we were so engrossed in our conversation that we totally missed the rest of our date. I would say that's a good thing."

He nodded his head. "You know, I don't think this has ever happened to me before."

That made her feel a lot better. Surely, Reed Sullivan had been out on many dates.

"Well, once we pay the check, you can just take me home."

He shook his head. "Absolutely not! Here we are, right by Waterfront Park, and you don't expect that I'm going to want to take a walk by the water with you?"

"I've never taken a walk at Waterfront Park. I've seen the fountain in pictures."

"You have to see it in person. Pictures don't do it justice. I can't let you go home without seeing it."

"Okay then. Waterfront Park, here we come!"

Shelby walked beside Reed along the water and felt like her stomach was in knots the whole time. How could she be in her forties now and still feel like a middle school girl whose crush had asked her to walk to class?

"Want to sit?" Reed asked as they passed yet another of the many benches the park offered. The breeze from the water pressed against her body, cooling it down on the warm summer night.

"Sure."

They sat down and faced the fountain, its beautiful lights bouncing around and creating a cascade of color. "How do you like the park?"

"It's… serene. That's the best word to describe it."

"Serene. I like it."

"So, I have to ask. Have you enjoyed our date?"

"Of course I have. Why wouldn't I?"

He shrugged his shoulders. His nice, broad shoulders. "I haven't always been the best judge of character, so I assume nothing."

"I get that."

"I know people in this town talk about me and how I've never been married. Apparently, that's a red flag."

She chuckled. "I've heard that's a possible red flag, yes."

"It's not because I don't want to be married. I do, actually. I want a family. The whole thing. Kids, dog, big yard. I just haven't found the right person, and I don't want to settle, you know? I see people settle. I don't mean settle for a person, but settle for a bad marriage."

"Like me?"

His eyes widened. "I didn't mean it that way, Shelby. Not at all."

"But I did settle."

"You didn't know that when you got married, I'm sure."

She scrunched her nose. "I think I did a little."

"You never had kids with him. Is that because the marriage was bad?"

"No. We tried for a very long time. It just didn't work, and then too much time had passed... biologically, I mean." Jeez, this was an embarrassing conversation to have on a first date.

"Did you want kids?"

"I did. Very much. To be honest, my ex-husband had some issues, and I believed marriage was forever. So, that meant no kids. And then my time ran out."

"Just because you're forty doesn't mean your time has run out."

"It feels that way. You have to understand, I'm starting completely over. No husband. No relationship. No career. I'm nowhere close to getting married and having kids, and by the time I am, if it ever happens, it'll be too late to have children."

She didn't know exactly why she was telling him this. It almost felt like a warning. As if this man was going to want to marry her. As if she was warning him away just in case he was looking for a perpetually fertile woman.

"Well, even if that happens, there are other ways to have kids. What about adoption?"

"I have considered it. I love children, and I'd like the opportunity to be somebody's mother."

"I've always wanted to adopt. My best friend was adopted, and I got to see firsthand just how amazing that was. His bond with his parents was no different from my bond with my parents. It's definitely not about genetics."

"I agree. I guess I'll just have to see what the future holds."

Reed laughed. "How do we get into these deep conversations?"

"I don't know. I thought we'd be talking about the weather or our favorite food."

"Well, what is your favorite food?"

"Anything at an Italian restaurant."

He chuckled. "And yet I took you to a French restaurant."

"I love French food, too. In fact, if I don't stop eating so much, I'm going to have to widen the doors of my new house."

He looked at her, those amazing blue eyes boring a hole straight through her skin. "I think you look just fine."

Shelby was glad it was dark outside, because he would've definitely seen her face blush.

Shelby sat at her kitchen table folding freshly dried towels. She loved her days off where she could just get some things done around the house and not have anything important to do. Today she had re-organized her pantry, put labels on her new spice jars, and now she was getting all of her laundry done.

Of course, all she could think about was her date with Reed last night. He'd been the perfect gentleman, simply kissing her hand when he walked her to her front door. Of course, she wouldn't have been opposed to him moving that kiss upward toward her lips.

After she finished folding her towels and putting them in the linen closet, Shelby went outside to do a little yard work. She had bought some new plants she wanted to put in the front flower bed, and she needed to water the ones she had planted last weekend.

She wasn't exactly a master gardener. Everything she learned had been from watching YouTube videos and reading gardening books at the bookstore. She was quite worried that it was too late in the season and way too hot to be planting things, but she was going to give it a shot, anyway.

"Those are beautiful!" Lacy yelled from across the street.

"Thanks! Just wanted to add some color to the front of the house."

Lacy walked closer, crossing the street and coming up the walkway. "I planted some of those in my back flower bed last year. They really bloomed nicely."

"I'm hoping these will do well. Have you been reading the book?"

"Of course. I always do my homework."

"Well, I wouldn't think of it as homework."

"So, the scuttlebutt on the street is that you went on a date with Reed Sullivan last night."

Shelby rolled her eyes and knelt down, pulling one plant out of the plastic container and loosening the roots. "Boy, gossip travels fast in this town."

"It does. How was it?" she asked, grinning.

"It was nice."

Lacy put her hands on her hips. "Nice? We're talking about Reed Sullivan! Every woman in town has tried to get him to commit for years."

"I'm not trying to get him to commit. I just went to dinner with him."

"And to Waterfront Park, from what I hear."

"Seriously, somebody was stalking me?"

"Oh, relax. My friend Daphne saw y'all. She was walking her dog."

"How did she know who I was?"

"She has seen you at the bookstore."

"Well, everybody can calm down because it was just a simple date. No big deal."

"Just be careful. Reed Sullivan has a reputation."

"A reputation for what?"

"Love them and leave them, from what I've heard."

"Maybe he's just never found the right person," Shelby said, digging into the dirt with her small shovel.

"Shelby, come on. What man in his forties hasn't found the right woman? There are plenty of fish in the sea."

"Well, maybe he's been fishing in the wrong ponds."

"Maybe so. I guess I'm just spoiled with how romantic my Ed was on our first dates."

"Oh yeah? What's the most romantic date you ever had with Ed?"

"Let me think… One time he picked me up, and he had prepared the most amazing picnic. But it started raining, so he decided that we would have an indoor picnic."

"That's it?"

"Not only did we have an indoor picnic, but we spent the entire night dancing under the starlight."

"The starlight? Inside?"

"Yes. He bought this lamp that put a cascade of stars all over the ceiling. We listened to Frank Sinatra while we swayed under the twinkling lights."

Shelby stood up and shook the dirt off her hands. "I guess that is pretty romantic."

"Yeah, it was," Lacy said, looking off into the distance like she was grieving for a moment.

"Is everything okay, Lacy?"

She snapped back and pasted on a smile. "Of course. Why wouldn't it be?"

"You just looked a little sad when you were talking about the good old days of dating."

She waved her hand toward Shelby. "It's no big deal. Every marriage waxes and wanes, you know?

We have little ones now, so romance isn't a high priority at the moment. It'll all come back around, I'm sure."

"Of course."

"Well, I'd better be going. I need to take some of Ed's shirts to the dry cleaner, pick up some snacks for Hazel's lunches, and finish some paperwork for the PTA."

Lacy's busy schedule made Shelby's head spin. "I'll see you at book club later this week, then?"

"I'll be there with bells on!"

Shelby was excited that it was time for book club again. She hadn't spoken to Joan since the day she came over to apologize, but she hoped that she would have something to say to the rest of the group.

As everybody filtered through the doorway, Shelby stood in the kitchen getting the coffee ready. She was getting accustomed to having these women around her. The first few days in Charleston had been quite lonely, but now she had a group of friends, although they were very different from one another.

Even Cami and Lacy seemed to be finally getting along somewhat. They still liked to verbally jab at each other from time to time, but it was nothing that Shelby couldn't handle. She found it quite humorous most of the time.

"I brought my grandma's famous macaroni and cheese," Cami said, walking into the kitchen and holding it up like she was showing off her new baby.

"Mac & cheese. One of my very favorite things to eat," Shelby said, taking the aluminum foil covered casserole dish from her and placing it on the kitchen island.

"And I brought my famous oatmeal raisin cookies. Before anybody says they don't like oatmeal raisin cookies, you haven't tried mine. There's a special ingredient!" Lacy said, setting her cookies on the other end of the counter.

"Unless the secret ingredient is an illicit drug that will make me forget I put on ten pounds in the last couple of months, I'm not interested," Cami said, rolling her eyes.

"Ten pounds? What have you been eating over there? Slabs of bacon?"

Maybe Shelby had spoken too soon. Would these two ever get along?

"If you must know, I've been under a lot of stress. Not having my husband at home is difficult," Cami said softly. Lacy looked at Shelby, a bit of guilt on her face.

"I understand."

Cami stared at her for a moment. "How would you understand? Your husband lives with you."

Lacy looked a little shaken and then laughed under her breath. "I mean, he just works so much that sometimes I forget he lives there."

There was an awkwardness that lingered in the air until Willadeene sauntered into the kitchen holding a covered dish. It was shocking because Willadeene rarely brought food to the book club meetings, even though she was supposed to.

"Where can I put this?"

"That depends. What is it?" Shelby asked.

"It's my famous pineapple grits casserole with crumbled cracker topping."

Lacy, Shelby and Cami all looked at each other. What on earth kind of mutant casserole was that going to be?

"Why don't you set it here beside the mac & cheese?" Shelby said, pasting on a smile. Cami leaned over closer to her ear.

"You'd better accidentally make sure that thing falls on the floor before any of us are forced to eat it."

"I know it sounds weird," Willadeene said loudly, "but my grandma made it, my mother made it, and I make it. It's always a hit."

"If you say so," Lacy said under her breath.

Willadeene wandered back out into the living

room, and Joan entered the kitchen at the same moment. "Hello, everyone."

"Joan, it's so good to see you. How's your mother?" Cami asked.

"She's doing well. I was able to find a caregiver that spends most of the day with her. Then she has some friends from church who are trading out time right now. I'll be going back in a few days."

"I'm glad to hear that."

There was a silence that fell over the room for a moment before Joan swallowed hard and spoke. "I've already apologized to Shelby, as I'm sure you've heard. I don't know what came over me the other night when you were just trying to help me, but I want to apologize to all of you."

"It's okay, Joan. We all understood," Cami said, glancing over at Lacy to make sure she stayed in line.

"I'm thankful to have you ladies. After so many years of being completely alone, it feels good to have a place in this neighborhood."

"What can we do to help you?" Lacy asked, surprising Shelby. She wasn't exactly the most caring individual on a regular basis, so she was glad to hear her ask Joan how they could help.

Joan clasped her hands together. "Well, that's why I wanted to talk to you before the meeting started. I was thinking about having a big yard sale. Getting rid of as much stuff as I can. Hiring a clean out crew, if I can afford it."

"I think that's a great idea," Shelby said.

"It's going to be very embarrassing for all the neighbors to see how much stuff I have. But it has to be done. I know it does. I can't keep living like this. It's not safe, and I'm not happy. Plus, there's a chance that my mother may have to come live with me, and I have nowhere for her to go."

"We will help you in whatever way we can. I used to do flea markets with my grandfather when I was a kid. I know how to organize and price everything," Cami said, walking over and taking one of Joan's hands.

Shelby walked closer and leaned across the countertop. "And I will help as much as I can. If you need somebody to help you haul trash away, I'll do it. I can help you get things organized in your house after the yard sale."

"Thank you, ladies. You'll never know how much I appreciate all of this."

Shelby looked over at Lacy, who was the only one who hadn't said anything about helping. "I'm great with yard sales, too. I would be glad to help."

Shelby was so happy to see how they were all coming together. They were all so very different, but most people needed the same things. Love, acceptance, friendship. She was happy to provide all of those to Joan.

Just as they were having such a nice moment, Willadeene poked her head back into the kitchen. "Are y'all going to get this show on the road or what?"

Shelby nodded her head. "Yes, Willadeene. We're coming," she groaned.

The women walked into the living room and sat down with everybody else. Over the last couple of weeks, a few more women from the neighborhood had shown up. Shelby was trying to remember their names, but she didn't know any of them very well just yet.

She was having a hard enough time keeping up with her new friends. And now the whole thing with Joan was occupying a lot of her brain space.

"Thanks for coming, everybody. I'm so excited to dig into the next two chapters. Did everybody have time to read them?"

"I actually read it this time!" Willadeene said. Shelby had noticed a change in her over the last week. She was waving at her in the yard, sometimes walking over to the property line and speaking. And tonight the fact that she got there on time, made food, and actually read the book was a big change.

"Very good, Willadeene! It sure makes the club more fun when you actually read the book." Everybody laughed, and Willadeene looked around, finally chuckling.

"I have to say that I really connected with these chapters," Cami said.

"In what way?"

"Our heroine is starting over, and that's really hard for her. She doesn't know who to trust. She doesn't know how to support herself. She misses her husband. I can relate to a lot of that, given that my husband is away right now."

"That must be hard," Shelby said.

"I started over when I came to this country many years ago. I understand what she feels as well," Daniela said. She didn't speak a lot during book club, but she seemed like a nice enough lady.

"Starting over is really difficult, whether it's from a divorce or a death. I think everybody deals with it differently. To me, it felt a little unrealistic that the heroine would be so strong," Joan said.

"What do you mean?" Lacy asked.

"I mean, she just comes right out of the gate being strong. Renovating a house, meeting the love of her life, taking over the local coffee shop. She doesn't seem to grieve the loss of her old life."

"Why should she grieve? The man cheated on her. He doesn't deserve one moment of her grief," Lacy said, leaning back in the chair and crossing her arms.

Joan looked up. "You can't help your grief, Lacy. It just happens, seeping into your life in a million different ways you don't expect until it happens to you."

"I just think women are stronger than that. I think we can pick ourselves up by our bootstraps and move on. Why let a man have a hold over you?"

"I don't think it's as cut and dry as all that. Women are strong. We rule the world from behind the scenes. But when you love somebody, and there's a risk that you're going to lose them, you'll do crazy things," Cami interjected.

"I would do anything to get my Andrew back. Literally anything," Joan said, wiping a tear from her cheek.

"Wow, this is getting way too heavy. Is it time to eat yet?" Willadeene suddenly asked.

Shelby looked over at her. "Honestly, Willadeene, we just got started. You need to eat a snack before you come over here next time."

CHAPTER 10

As book club - and the very deep conversations - wrapped up for the night, Shelby invited everyone into the kitchen to eat. She enjoyed the time they had together, chatting and trying everyone's food. Cami's mac and cheese was amazing, of course. It was hard to screw up mac and cheese, anyway.

Then there were Daniela's stuffed mushrooms. Shelby didn't know what kind of cheese was in those, but they were heavenly. Lacy's oatmeal raisin cookies were the best Shelby had ever had. Then there was Willadeene's casserole. Everybody bypassed it as long as they could, but Willadeene wasn't having that.

"Nobody is leaving this house until you all try my casserole," she said, crossing her arms and standing in the doorway.

"I'm actually quite full," Lacy said, putting her hand on her tiny abdomen. Shelby tried to imagine what she'd looked like pregnant. It didn't seem anatomically possible that she'd given birth to three kids.

"I don't care," Willadeene said, squinting her eyes. "It's good. I swear. My whole family has eaten it for years."

Cami leaned over the casserole like she was a coroner, about to examine a body. She tilted her head. "What are the black things?"

"Raisins, of course."

Lacy put her hand over her mouth like she was about to vomit. "Oh darn! I'm deathly allergic to raisins."

Willadeene looked down at Lacy's plate. "Then why have you polished off two of your own oatmeal raisin cookies in the last ten minutes?"

"Fine! I don't want to eat your casserole. I was trying to be kind, but you've left me no choice but to tell the truth."

Willadeene stood there for a moment and then walked straight over to Lacy. She waved her closer, leaned into Lacy's ear, and whispered something nobody else could hear. Lacy's face fell as she listened, and then Willadeene stepped back, a satisfied smile on her face.

"What was that about?" Cami asked.

"You know, on second thought, I believe I will have a piece of Willadeene's casserole. It'd be rude not to, right?" As the room fell into an eerie silence, Lacy walked over, scooped out a glob of the casserole, and plopped it onto her white dessert place. She took a bite, her jaw clenching with every chew.

"Well, how is it?" Willadeene asked.

"Mmmm… It's just delightful," Lacy said, obviously forcing a smile.

Shelby decided she'd have to ask Lacy later what Willadeene whispered because it must've been something else for it to have made Lacy eat even one bite of that casserole.

Just as Willadeene was about to set her sights on everyone else, a barrage of dings created a cacophony of sound across the kitchen. Everyone reached into their purses and pockets, pulling out their cell phones.

"What is it?" Shelby asked. Her phone was charging upstairs on her nightstand.

"Some kind of warning about an escaped convict," Lacy said, staring at her phone. "And he looks quite frightening." She held her phone out toward Shelby.

"Well, to be fair, nobody looks their best in a mug shot."

"Seriously, though, he looks like he could rip your face off in an instant. I need to go home and relieve the babysitter. I don't like the idea of this maniac being loose."

"Your husband isn't home taking care of the kids?" Shelby asked.

"Oh, no, he had a late meeting. I'll see you ladies later!" Lacy bolted out of the front door as if her kids were being specifically targeted by a serial killer.

"Well, I hope it's not some murderer," Willadeene said. "I have valuables in my house, you know."

"Like what?" Shelby asked.

"My mother's china, for one thing. Oh, and a bunch of those collector dolls you buy on TV. I even have all the certificates of authenticity."

Shelby didn't want to burst her bubble by telling her none of those things would be of interest to a real criminal. "Just keep your doors locked, and I'm sure you'll be fine."

"He's not a murderer," Cami suddenly said.

"How do you know?" Willadeene asked.

"Because it says so on the notification." She held up her phone and pointed. "Looks like he was incarcerated for drug charges."

"Must've been a lot of drugs to be put away in prison. I'm assuming he's not your typical druggie out on the streets with a couple of joints. This guy sounds like the real deal, which means he's going to be desperate to stay out of prison. Desperate people are dangerous."

Cami rolled her eyes. "Oh, Willadeene, you're so dramatic sometimes. I'm sure the police will catch him in no time. Listen, I need to get home. I promised to teach a private yoga class in the morning to a very rich client."

"Sounds exciting," Shelby said, hugging her good-bye. Cami was the most affectionate out of their group, and Shelby loved hugs.

"Yes, it's a great opportunity to make some extra money. Well, I'll see y'all later."

"Be careful! Remember, there's a psycho on the loose!" Willadeene called.

As everybody left and went home, Shelby noticed Willadeene was hanging around. First, she offered to help clean up the kitchen, and then she just planted herself on Shelby's loveseat.

"Is there some reason you're hanging around? I don't mean to be rude, but I'm pretty tired."

"Well, I'm not super excited about going home when there's a convict on the loose."

"I'm sure everything is going to be fine. What are the odds a convict is going to show up in this neighborhood? He would stick out like a sore thumb, anyway."

"I had something else I wanted to talk to you about."

Shelby sat across from her on the sofa, slapping her hands on her knees. "Okay, what is it?" She really

just wanted to get to the bottom of whatever
Willadeene wanted to talk about so she could go
to bed.

"It's about Lacy. She's keeping some secrets, and I
know at least one of them. That's how I got her to
eat my casserole."

"Secrets?"

"She likes to play it off like she has this big, happy
family and perfect marriage. But things are not what
they seem with Ed."

"What do you mean?"

"What I mean is that he doesn't really live there
anymore."

"What? That's crazy."

"Crazy but true."

"And how do you know that?"

"For one thing, you don't see him during the
daytime."

"Lacy has already told us he works long hours. Of
course, he wouldn't be at the house in the middle of
the day."

"And have you noticed she always has a
babysitter?"

"Again, her husband works late hours. What are
you getting at?"

"Come with me," Willadeene said, standing up
and pointing toward the front door. She opened it

and walked outside, crouching behind some of the big bushes in front of Shelby's porch.

"What are you doing?"

"Get down before she sees us!" Willadeene said, grabbing Shelby's arm and pulling her down.

"This is crazy, even for you."

"I'm an old lady with nothing more to do than watch the neighborhood, and I noticed something recently."

"Okay, what?"

"Every evening, Ed comes home for dinner. I see them through the window at the table with their little kids."

"I think that's called stalking."

"Then they shut their drapes. Anyway, he comes home for dinner and then, about this time of night, he leaves."

"So?"

"Even when the babysitter is there, he's there. And at this time, right after it gets dark, he leaves."

"Willadeene, why is any of this important?"

"Every night, Shelby. I've been tracking it for almost two months now. The same routine. Eat dinner, put the kids to bed, he leaves out the side door with a duffel bag."

Shelby had to admit that was a bit suspicious. Where was he going every night? Obviously Lacy

had to know since he didn't sleep in the bed
with her.

"Maybe he has another job."

Willadeene turned and looked at her. "Seriously?
The man makes massive amounts of money as an
attorney. He's one of the best in town. I'm sure he's
not working on the side at the local seven-eleven."

"Then what do you think is going on?"

"I think there's trouble in paradise. Lacy wants us
to think she has a perfect marriage, but what she
really has is a broken one."

Shelby stood up. "It's really none of our business
what's going on in someone's marriage. People were
always gossiping about mine before we got divorced,
and it didn't feel good. I say leave this alone and
don't say a word to Lacy."

"She talks a big game all the time about being a
strong woman and having this happy marriage.
Doesn't it bother you she's been lying to us?"

Shelby turned and walked toward her front door.
"No. Because it's none of my business. And it's none
of your business. Go home, Willadeene."

She walked into her house and shut the door
behind her, locking it. At this point, she wasn't sure
if she was locking out the convict or Willadeene.

~

"Stop parking right under the streetlight. It's only a matter of time before somebody sees you."

Ed crossed his arms over his chest. "So now you're telling me where to park?"

"Look, I didn't want this. It's your actions that put you in this position."

"Seriously, Lacy? There are indiscretions in people's marriages all the time, and they don't handle it like this."

She popped the cork off a bottle of wine and poured herself a glass, leaning against the kitchen counter. "Well, this is how *we're* handling it."

"I made a mistake. One time. You know our marriage hasn't been right for the last couple of years."

"Well, it didn't stop you from getting me pregnant multiple times. If you thought our marriage was in the dumper, then maybe you should've taken greater care to make sure that didn't happen. As far as I knew, our marriage was great."

He sighed. "You can't really say that with a straight face. You know you kept your own secret for a long time."

"That was self-preservation."

"Call it whatever you want. You know I will not keep doing this forever."

"It's time to go, Ed." She walked over to the side

door of the kitchen and opened it. "Next time, park over here. Stay away from the streetlight."

He slowly walked toward the door, turning toward her. "How long is this going to go on?"

"Well, our youngest is two years old. So, I'd say maybe about sixteen more years?"

"I'm not doing that. I'm going to talk to my attorney tomorrow. Either we're going to work this out, or I'm moving on."

"Seems like you deciding to move on is what started this whole situation in the first place."

He leaned closer to her face. "I've let you do all of this because I know I deserve to be punished, but I'm done. I will have unfettered access to my kids. I will have a normal lifestyle. If you want to live in this dysfunction, you go right ahead. But I won't let my kids suffer through this anymore."

"You know as well as I do that they have no idea what's going on."

"They're getting older, and they're not stupid. Hazel told me the other day that she got up in the middle of the night with a bad dream and noticed that I wasn't there in the bed with you."

"She did?"

"Yes, she did. I will not risk the mental health of my kids, Lacy. This needs to get resolved one way or another."

He turned and walked out the door, Lacy shutting it slowly and then leaning against it. She'd been strong her whole life, but it was times like this when she wanted to just break down into a million pieces. It was her strength that kept her going, and it was also her strength that kept her stuck.

Shelby, Lacy and Cami had spent all morning at Joan's house helping her get organized for the yard sale. Going through all of her stuff had been difficult, to say the least. There were many things that Joan wasn't ready to let go of, either because she thought they were worth more money or because they reminded her of her late husband.

Shelby kept having to have conversations with her about what she wanted. What kind of life did she want to live? What kind of space did she want in her house? Where would she put her mother if she came to live with her?

In the end, Joan let go of a lot. They were able to fill the garage with tables and stacks of merchandise for the yard sale tomorrow. There was still a lot of stuff that Joan wasn't totally ready to go through, mostly her husband's possessions. So, they moved those things into her storage closet.

"I'm pooped!" Lacy said, falling down onto the newly uncovered living room sofa. It was outdated, for sure, but Joan was delighted to have somewhere to sit.

"I can't thank you all enough for coming over and helping me. There's no way I could've gotten ready for this yard sale by myself."

"You're going to make a ton of money," Cami said, smiling. "Think of the renovations you can do with the money you're going to make."

"I am looking forward to that. I've always wanted to have a covered back porch. And I'd like to put in some new flower gardens in the spring."

"You'll be able to do all of that and more," Shelby said, patting her on the back.

"Sometimes I wonder what Andrew would think if he could see this house right now. How I've let it go. How I've lived in squalor for the last few years."

"Your husband would understand. I'm sure he had something to do with us finding out so that you could get the help you need."

"Maybe so," she said, smiling as she ran her fingers across their wedding photo that was on a nearby shelf.

"Has anybody heard anything else about that convict?" Lacy suddenly asked.

"No. I know they're still looking for him, but that's about it," Shelby said.

"I don't think he's anything to worry about. Just

drug offenses," Cami said as she folded a quilt that was draped over the arm of the couch.

"Yeah, but people will do anything to get their drugs. That's usually how it starts, you know. Criminals almost always start with drugs."

Cami slammed a box she was holding onto the floor. Thankfully, it only had books in it. Everyone turned and looked at her. "Do you realize how incredibly judgmental that sounds?"

"I don't think it's judgmental at all. It's truthful. People often start their criminal lives by taking or selling drugs. I mean, has anyone watched an episode of Cops around here?"

"Ladies, that's really not what this day is about. Let's try to focus on helping Joan get everything priced for the yard sale tomorrow. We don't have many more hours before we will have to call it quits for the night."

"You're right. This is not the time for me to drive myself insane having a conversation with Lacy," Cami said, turning around and picking up the box of books. "I apologize, Joan."

"It's okay. I totally understand. And I agree with you, Cami. Stereotypes are never a good thing."

"Well, I guess I'm getting shamed," Lacy said, throwing her hands in the air. She turned back to a box she was working on and quietly sorted through it.

"Is anybody hungry? I could order up some food." Shelby was starving and ready to break the tension in the room.

"I'm starving, but please, not pizza. I don't think I can stand another one. I've been ordering them a lot lately," Cami said.

"And no Chinese. I simply can't handle the MSG," Lacy said, scrunching up her nose.

"Well, the only place open at this hour is probably going to be Graystone."

Lacy giggled. "Oh, Graystone. And I'm sure that has nothing to do with the owner."

"It has nothing to do with that. I don't even think he's working tonight," Shelby said, shaking her head while she totally lied. She knew Reed was working, and she wanted to see him.

"I don't mind going and picking it up," Cami offered.

"No, that's fine," Shelby said, waving her hand. "Everybody text me your orders, and I will call it in on my way over there." Before anybody could argue with her, she slipped out the side door and headed for her car.

Shelby stood at the front, craning her head every so often to see if she saw Reed. Maybe he really wasn't working tonight. Maybe he had left early to take some other woman on a date.

Before she could think of any other terrible scenarios, Reed came walking over from the kitchen.

"Shelby! What a nice surprise! What are you doing here?"

"I ordered dinner, actually."

He picked up a bag from the shelf behind him. "This must be yours. Wow, this is a lot of food. Are you just really hungry?"

Shelby laughed. "I'm hungry, but not *that* hungry. I'm actually helping a friend tonight. She's getting ready for a yard sale tomorrow, so a few of us ladies in the neighborhood are helping organize."

"Oh, that's really nice. She must have a lot of stuff."

"Yeah, we actually found out that she's been living as a hoarder. We've done a lot of work there today. I'm pretty exhausted, which explains why I've shown up at your restaurant sweaty again."

He smiled. "That's a very nice thing you're doing. I had an uncle who was a hoarder. He died that way. Cleaning out his property was a nightmare."

"We're hoping to help Joan have a better life. She lost her husband a few years ago, and this was how she dealt with her grief. Very sad."

"Does she have a lot of good things to sell?"

"Surprisingly, yes. She and her husband had a

thrifting and reselling business for many years. She's got some cool stuff."

"Well, good luck with the yard sale."

"Thanks," she said, taking the large brown paper bag out of his hand and turning toward the door.

"It was good to see you. Maybe we can get together again soon?"

She turned around and smiled. "I certainly hope so."

CHAPTER 11

Early mornings were one of Shelby's least favorite things. Real estate had allowed her to have a flexible schedule, and one of her rules was never to see the outside of her house before nine AM, and even that was pushing it.

After all the work the day before and then a late dinner with the girls, she was running on fumes. But today was the yard sale, and hopefully they would get rid of a lot of stuff for Joan. Starting at seven in the morning had been Lacy's bright idea, and she was planning to get revenge on her later.

The entire driveway and front yard were covered in tables, each one holding stacks of merchandise, vintage items and just regular yard sale stuff. There was stuff on the ground, in buckets and in boxes.

So far, they had been going for about an hour,

and Shelby was certain that most of Charleston had walked across Joan's driveway at some point. She didn't even know how much money Joan had made so far, but she seemed giddy with excitement as each thing was taken away to a new home.

"How are you feeling?" Shelby asked Joan as she sat down beside her in one of the folding chairs.

"At first I was a little anxious about it. These things have surrounded me since my husband died, and as weird as it is to say, they were my company. Now there's a bit of a void inside my house."

"Well, that void is there so that you can fill it with something good. Something happy. Like your new neighbor friends."

Joan smiled. "I'm feeling much more encouraged and excited about the future now. I don't feel so alone anymore."

"You're not alone."

Joan looked up across the yard. "Wow. Look at that guy! He looks like a cover model."

Shelby turned her head and noticed Reed walking across the yard toward her, a big smile on his face. He had a brown bag in his hand and a carrier with several coffees in the other hand.

"Reed? What are you doing here?"

"I just thought you ladies could use a little sustenance. I brought our famous blueberry muffins, a couple of breakfast sandwiches, and some coffee. You can split it up however you like."

Like moths to a flame, Lacy and Cami came trotting over when they saw Reed in the yard.

"Hey, I'm Lacy. I've been to your restaurant before. Very good. Had the lobster bisque, and I have to say it's the best in town," she said, reaching out her hand to shake his.

"Glad to hear you enjoyed it."

"Hi, I'm Cami. I haven't been to your restaurant yet, but I'm looking forward to it."

"Nice to meet you. I hope you like it when you come."

"I'm sure I will," Cami said, winking at Shelby.

"I was just telling Shelby that I brought some breakfast for you ladies. You can divvy it up however you want," he said, setting it on the table in front of Joan and Shelby. They were sitting in front of the cash box, taking money from buyers.

"Thank you, really. That was very thoughtful of you."

"Is there anything I can help with?"

Shelby tilted her head to the side. "Aren't you heading to work?"

He laughed. "I own the place, Shelby. I have people for that. I thought maybe you had some stuff here you needed moved or something you needed help with? I'm pretty handy."

"I suppose you could help bring out some more boxes from the house. I mean, as long as you don't judge my... situation," Joan said.

He smiled, his dimples becoming more prominent. "I'm not the type of person who would judge anyone. I have my own skeletons, just like everyone else."

"This is the first I'm hearing about any skeletons," Shelby said, laughing.

"That's more third date conversation," he said, winking. Dang, when he winked, it made her knees feel weak.

"Well, if you don't mind helping, there's a stack just inside the sunporch. The blue totes."

"I'll go get them!"

As Reed walked away, all three women turned their attention toward Shelby, each one of them grinning like a Cheshire cat.

"Wow. I've heard how good-looking he is, but it really is something you have to see in person," Joan said, laughing as she took a muffin from the bag.

"Yes, he's very attractive," Shelby said, trying to sound unbothered.

"He is smitten with you, girl!" Cami said, lightly punching her arm.

"You think so?"

Her mouth dropped open. "You can't tell? Has it really been that long since you dated? That man is head over heels or he wouldn't be here this early in the morning to bring you breakfast."

Shelby rolled her eyes. "He brought all of us breakfast."

"I hate to agree with Cami, but that man would not come over here to bring us breakfast unless you were here. He's got a thing for you," Lacy said as she snatched one of the breakfast sandwiches and broke it in half, offering the other half to Cami.

Shelby smiled. "I kind of hope so. It's the first time I have ever felt this way about someone, and it's pretty scary. I mean, he's never been married and every woman in town would love to snag him. I've never dated anyone that good-looking."

"You should have more confidence in yourself. You're a great person, and a beautiful woman. You deserve someone who will treat you right. You deserve someone who will make you feel the way your husband should've made you feel all those years," Cami said.

"Thank you." Before she could say anything else, Reed reappeared with an enormous stack of plastic totes. He slowly put them down on the ground and let out a deep breath.

"Those were heavier than I thought."

Joan laughed. "Sorry about that. I can't remember what's in them. Must be books."

"No problem. I don't have to go to the gym this morning since I'm getting my workout here."

"You don't have to stay," Shelby said quietly. Thankfully, Lacy and Cami had wandered off into the yard to help customers who had questions about pricing.

"I don't mind. You're doing a good thing here, and spending my morning with you sounds like a great idea to me."

Sensing she was out of place, Joan slipped away to talk to another neighbor. Shelby felt heat rising up her neck and into her face, her cheeks probably turning red.

"I didn't expect to see you here this morning."

He slid into the chair next to her where Joan had been sitting. "I wanted it to be a surprise. Here, try one of these muffins."

He reached his hand into the bag and handed her a blueberry muffin. She took a bite of it, starving.

"Oh, my gosh! I've never had a muffin so good. Did you come up with this recipe?"

"Of course. I come up with all the recipes at my restaurant. I coordinate with my pastry chef on some things, but these are all me."

She picked up a napkin and dabbed at the corner of her mouth. "You should publish a cookbook. You're really amazing at what you do."

"And you're just amazing," he said, softly.

"Stop making me blush!"

"Okay, okay. It's just that I haven't ever dated someone quite like you."

She turned and looked at him. "Are we dating?"

"Well, in that we have been on a date, then I'd say we're dating." She wanted to ask if they were exclusive, but it seemed too soon. Too presumptuous.

"I think to be dating, you have to go on multiple dates."

His eyebrows raised. "Oh yeah? Are you asking me out, Shelby Anderson?"

"Only if you promise to say yes."

He leaned over, his lips barely an inch from her earlobe. "Yes."

Now she understood all those movies where southern belles fanned themselves. Handsome southern gentlemen were the source of the heat.

Joan stood in her newly cleaned out house, amazed by how much they got rid of in such a short amount of time. She was so thankful for the new friends she'd met at book club. Who knew that simply taking the chance of going to a book club meeting could lead to something like this?

She walked around, looking at her carpet, her hardwood floors, her walls. These were things she hadn't seen in years. She saw the gouge on the hard-wood floor where Andrew had dropped a jar of mayonnaise. She saw the wall where their wedding picture had once hung but had fallen down over the years.

There was a part of her that also felt sad that some of her things were gone. Over the years, those things had been her company. Her constant companions. Stability. Now it was time to build a new life.

With the money she'd made from the yard sale, she would have a nice amount in savings, but she'd also be able to do some maintenance items around the house. Reed Sullivan had even offered to do a few of the things himself. From what she could understand, he was pretty handy, not to mention nice to look at. If she was going to hire a contractor, he might as well be attractive.

Watching him with Shelby reminded her of the early days with Andrew. The flirty glances. The stolen moments. She missed her husband with every fiber of her being, but that chapter had closed. She knew it was time to move on, whatever that looked like.

She sat down on the sofa, her cell phone in her hand, knowing the next thing she needed to do. There was no getting around it, and it was time to face it.

"Okay, here goes." She dialed the number and listened to it ring, partially hoping for someone to answer, and partially hoping it'd go to voicemail.

"Hello?" The sound of her son's voice was unmistakable. Somehow it seemed deeper now, although she knew it wasn't. He had the same rasp in his voice that his father had.

"Hey, son."

She had expected for the line to go dead and her son to hang up on her, but there was just silence for a moment. "Mom?"

At least he still called her mom. "Yes, it's me."

"Why are you calling?" The monotone sound of his voice let her know he was still not interested in talking to her, but she would not give up.

"I know it's a surprise that I'm calling you right now, but I miss you."

"Look, I know you want us to have a relationship, but I can't watch what you're doing to your life and to the house."

"You mind if I send you a photo while we're on the phone?"

"A photo? What is this all about?"

"Just humor me for a moment, okay? I'm sending the photo now."

A few moments later, she could hear his phone ding, signaling the text message's arrival. It was quiet for a minute.

"So you hired somebody to clean your house?"

"No. I did it with my new friends."

"New friends? You haven't spoken to people in years."

"I know, and that was wrong. I joined a book club in my neighborhood with some other women, and they sort of found out that I had a hoarding problem. They helped me. We cleaned out the house and had a big yard sale yesterday. The rest of it will get thrown away, donated, or taken to the consignment store."

"Is it just the living room?

"No. We went through the whole house. I still have a few of your father's things that I don't want to get rid of, so they are in the storage closet, but otherwise, everything is gone."

"Wow. I didn't expect that."

"I'm making some changes in my life, son. One of those changes is that I'd like for you to be a part of it again. I'd like to prove to you I can be who I once was. Well, maybe not who I once was. I don't think she exists without your father. But I could be a new, better version of myself."

"I don't know…"

"Please, just keep an open mind. Give me a chance. I'm going to start counseling soon, and I'm also going to look for a job."

"Are you having money problems?"

"No. But I need to get out of this house and do something worthwhile."

"I'm glad you're doing all of this, for your sake. I just don't know if it's too late for us."

A tear rolled down her cheek, and she wiped it away. "It's never too late for a mother and her child. I've made some big mistakes, but I've learned that I deserve more than what I've been giving myself all these years. Your father wouldn't have wanted this for me."

"You're right about that."

"Your grandmother has been ill. I'm going out to see her in a few days. I'd love it if you'd come too."

"I can't. I have work, and I have my son."

Her breath caught in her throat. "Your son?"

"Lila and I had a baby last June. He just turned a year old."

She paused for a moment. "So, I'm a grandma?"

"I suppose so."

Joan's eyes filled with tears. "Can I meet him sometime?"

Her son said nothing for a long moment. "I'll talk to Lila. Maybe we can come visit soon."

She wanted to jump for joy and scream as loud as she could, but she thought better of it. Her son might think she was insane.

"I would love that."

"Okay. Well, I need to go. We're taking Andy to the park."

"Andy? You named him Andy after your dad?"

"His name is Andrew Michael. We call him Andy."

"Your father would be so proud of you."

"Thanks. Goodbye, Mom."

"Goodbye."

She pressed end and sat there staring through the front window for a moment. She had a grandson. She was a grandma. This truly was her second chance, and she would not waste it.

"I don't know if this counts as an actual date," Shelby said, stirring the spaghetti noodles on her stove top.

After a long morning working at the garage sale, Reed had gone to work for a little while and come back. By late afternoon, they were closing everything down, and both of them were starving.

Shelby had invited him over for a spaghetti dinner, which was a risky thing to do, given that he was a world-class chef. Her experience with cooking involved opening a lot of boxes and jars, adding salt and pepper and calling it a meal.

"If we're together, it's a date."

She laughed. "So I guess the garage sale was a date?"

"Yes. So let's call this our third date? Fourth?"

"I've lost count," she said, turning the heat off on the noodles and pulling a colander from the cabinet.

"Are you sure I can't help you?"

"I'm sure. You definitely do not want your name associated with this meal."

"I told you we could go to the restaurant."

"Oh no, you're not getting out of it now! I'm about to show you my cooking skills, and then you'll have a reason to never have to go on a date with me again."

He walked across the kitchen and took a bottle of wine from the counter, opening drawers until he found the corkscrew. "I don't want a reason to get away from you," he said, walking behind her and poking her in the side.

"Okay, just remember that when you take your first bite of this spaghetti."

Shelby got the Parmesan cheese out of the refrigerator and put it on the kitchen table. Reed took the salad out of the refrigerator along with a bottle of ranch dressing and brought it over to the table.

She was amazed at how well they worked together, like they'd been cooking with each other for years. She imagined that if he'd cooked this meal, it would taste amazing, while hers tasted mediocre.

"I hope you like garlic. I put a lot of garlic in my sauce," she said, stirring it one last time before she turned off the heat.

"I love garlic. I'm a chef."

"No, I don't think you understand my love of garlic. Like if garlic was a person, I would be engaged to it."

He walked closer, his face a few inches from hers. "But not married? That means I still have a chance."

"Yeah, you're probably not going to want to be this close after I eat this spaghetti. But at least I'll scare any vampires away."

"Why do you keep trying to run me off?"

"Because you scare me a little."

"Scare you? Why?"

She pushed the sauce to the back of the stove and leaned against the counter. "Because I don't know your intentions."

"My intentions?"

"You know you're probably the best-looking guy in town. You're single, and every woman wants to date you. I guess I just don't understand why you're pursuing me."

His eyebrows furrowed together. "First of all, I don't think I'm the best-looking guy in town. Not even close. And I don't pay any attention to who might want to date me. I think you're overestimating that."

"That's cute that you think that, but it's not true."

"Look, I don't know what kind of mental games your ex-husband played with you, but you're a beautiful woman. You're smart, funny. You're a catch. As far as I'm concerned, I'm the lucky one to be even getting to sit down tonight and have dinner with you. You scare me a little, too."

She smiled. "Really?"

"Really," he said, softly. "And on second thought, I am a bit worried about that garlic. I'm thinking it's safer to kiss you now."

Before she could say anything else, he slid his hand around to the base of her head and pulled her lips to his. And then she didn't remember much. There were fireworks and the sound of her heartbeat in her ears. There was warmth and movement and energy zipping up and down her body.

When he pulled away, she sucked in for air, realizing she'd been holding her breath the whole time.

"Was that okay?"

Shelby laughed. "Oh, that was more than okay."

"Good. Now, let's taste your spaghetti."

"Well, it was fun while it lasted," Shelby mumbled to herself, figuring once he tasted her cooking, he'd run straight back home.

CHAPTER 12

SHELBY SAT AT ONE OF THE LITTLE TABLES IN THE bookstore, leafing through some of the new books that had come in. She loved to read, and lately she didn't have nearly as much time to do it. She was always busy at work, doing book club, or helping Joan finish cleaning out her house.

Turned out, she had more stuff in the attic but didn't want to go through the hassle of another yard sale. They had been sorting through it, taking some of it to a consignment store and selling other items on a local online marketplace.

This morning, though, Shelby had some free time. It was raining outside, which meant a lot fewer people were coming into the bookstore. Nobody was walking around out on the street doing any window shopping, after all.

Reed had gone out of town for a couple of days on business. He was checking out some new vendors for different food products, always trying to innovate at the restaurant. After their last date, he'd asked if she wanted to date exclusively, to which she'd said yes, of course. Things were moving faster than she'd thought they would, but it all just felt right.

She pulled the next book from the stack, bored by the other three she had tried to read. This one was a little different from what she normally read. She would classify it as steamy romance, and that was something she didn't normally pick up. The cover on this one looked pretty good, like it had some suspense too, so she figured she'd give it a go.

For the next thirty minutes, she found herself enthralled by the book. It really pulled her in, and she loved the author's writing style. She had never heard of Jasmine Cain before, which was unusual since she was such an avid reader.

She pulled up the author's website and saw that she had ten books. Shelby decided she might order some of the other ones if she liked this one as much as she thought she was going to. It wasn't just a steamy romance, but more of a psychological thriller with some romance thrown in.

Before she knew it, she was three chapters in and completely addicted. This author knew how to write in a way that made her never want to put the book down until it was over.

It wasn't until she got to the beginning of chapter four, while reading a description of the first date of the couple in the book, that she got a funny feeling in her stomach. Why did this sound so familiar? The description was something she had heard before, and she worried that this author had plagiarized someone else.

Plagiarism was a big pet peeve of hers. She hated when people copied other people. Surely this author wouldn't have done that. She kept reading, and every part seemed so familiar to her. If she had read it in another book, she certainly couldn't remember which one.

Eventually, a customer came in, forcing Shelby to put down the book for a little while. She helped the woman find a book on studying for the LSAT exam and then talked to her for a little while about her experience at law school. Shelby was always interested in everybody's story.

She was about to pick the book up again when another customer arrived, asking about middle grade children's books. The woman was a teacher and wanted something for the book club she was forming for the kids. She spent quite a while going through different options with the teacher before she left the store.

By the time Shelby sat down to read the book again, it was time to start the closing process. Using her employee discount, she purchased the book so she could read it more at home. She counted out the register, turned off the lights, and locked the door behind her, stepping out into the humid Charleston evening.

Thankfully, the rain had stopped a couple of hours before, so she didn't have to walk through a downpour. Her car was one block over because of the roadwork they were doing.

"Shelby?"

She turned around to see Lacy standing outside the local sushi place. "Oh, hey. Grabbing some dinner?"

"Yeah. Just needed a little comfort food."

Shelby laughed. "You consider sushi to be comfort food? I was thinking more about chicken pot pie or mashed potatoes."

Lacy waved her hand. "Oh, dear, you can't eat those things all the time. You know what they say, a moment on the lips, a lifetime on the hips."

"I don't think that's scientifically accurate."

"Heading home?"

"Yes. I'm going to eat some leftover pizza I have in the fridge, and read a good book," she said, pulling the book out of her tote bag.

Lacy looked at it. "Have you started reading it?"

"Yes. I couldn't stop. It's truly a page turner."

"I didn't realize you read books like that."

"Are you judging me?"

"Of course not. That just looks a little sexier than I expected."

Shelby laughed. "Believe it or not, there's some fantastic writing in here. Suspense, twists, and turns. I like it so far."

"Are you planning to use it for book club?"

"Oh, I doubt it. If Willadeene read this, I think her head would explode."

Lacy laughed. "Well, I'd better get home. The sitter is keeping the kids, but she has plans tonight and needs to leave soon."

"Hey, Lacy?"

"Yeah?" she said, turning around.

"Can I ask you something?"

"Sure."

"It seems like your husband is never there at night and you always have a sitter. It's none of my business, but I'm just wondering if everything is okay?"

She smiled. "Everything is fine. My husband is a very busy man, that's all."

Shelby didn't know if she bought that excuse, but she didn't want to push it. Lacy was still a very new friend, and it wasn't really any of Shelby's business. Her curiosity was just getting the best of

her after Willadeene's crazy notions the other
night.

"Glad to hear it. I guess I'll see you at book club."

"See you then," Lacy said before slipping into her
large SUV and driving away. Shelby couldn't put her
finger on it, but she felt like Lacy's secrets were
rising to the surface, and she was desperate to
contain them.

It was book club night again, and Shelby was excited
to talk about the end of the book they'd been reading. She had really enjoyed it, although she had had a
problem forcing herself to read it instead of Jasmine
Cain's books.

She had become obsessed with that author's
books and hoped that the book club would read one
in the future. For now, she had to focus on the
current book and getting the rest of the food ready.
Tonight would be their last meeting about that book,
so they would have some time to vote on a new book
before the next session of the book club started.

"Are you worried about Cami?" Lacy asked,
standing in the kitchen next to Shelby as she
prepared banana pudding.

"Very worried. She hasn't been to our last two
meetings, and when I went over there, she didn't

even answer the door. I finally got her to return a text."

"What did she say?"

"She told me she's fine, just overwhelmed with work and dealing with some personal issues. She insists she will be back soon."

"Well, I guess we have to take her at her word."

Shelby wiped down the kitchen counter. "Or we could go over there and force her to tell us what's going on."

"I don't think that's a good idea. When people want privacy, you need to give it to them."

"Not necessarily. She's our friend. If something is going on and she's too embarrassed to tell us, then we might need to get pushy."

Lacy turned and leaned against the counter. "Look, I know you're one of those types that wants to help everybody, but sometimes people want to handle things privately. On their own. "

Shelby couldn't help but wonder if Lacy felt that way about her own life. She obviously had issues going on in her personal life that she didn't want anyone else to know about.

Shelby had looked out the window several nights over the last couple of weeks and noticed that Willadeene was right. Every single night, Lacy's husband left. And he didn't come home until sometime the next day. He was usually only there for a short time, and then he was gone again.

It occurred to Shelby that nobody worked that much. Something was going on, but she had no idea what it was.

"So how are things going with Mr. Handsome?" Lacy asked, smiling. It was obvious she was changing the subject.

"He was out of town for a bit, but he's back. We've gone out to dinner a few times. Things are going really well, actually."

"Do you think he's the one?"

Shelby laughed. "I don't know if I believe that there's only one person for each of us. But I think things are getting pretty serious. I could see some-thing long-term with him."

"Have you fallen in love, Shelby?" she teased.

Shelby thought about that question. She had never really been in love before, even though she'd had a long marriage. After she got out of her marriage, she realized it wasn't real love she had felt for Roger. She didn't trust herself to know what that felt like. But things with Reed were very different. And the only way she could describe that feeling would be love.

"It's way too soon to be professing love," she said, pulling coffee mugs out of the cabinet. "Now, let's get out there because I think I just heard someone come in."

"Saved by the bell," Lacy said under her breath as they walked out of the kitchen.

Shelby stood in the middle of the darkened room, Frank Sinatra playing on the TV. Candles were lit all over the room. Reed held her waist and swayed to the music, his lips trailing up and down her neck. She felt shivers up her spine as he...

Knock, knock, knock!

Shelby bolted upright in her bed, her heart pounding. She grabbed the baseball bat from under her bed and crept out onto the landing at the top of the stairs.

"Shelby! Answer the door!" She recognized Willadeene's voice immediately and ran down the stairs, trying not to slip in her socked feet.

"Willadeene, what on earth are you doing? It's two o'clock in the morning!"

Willadeene, wearing the ugliest housecoat ever made, pushed past her and into the house. She ran straight to the living room and sat on the sofa, breathless.

"He's in my house!"

Shelby closed the door and locked it. "Who's in your house?"

"A ghost!"

"Oh, dear Lord, Willadeene! I thought something was actually wrong. Go home and go to bed. You had a bad dream, is all."

"No, I didn't! I woke up to get a drink of water, and I could hear him upstairs in the attic. Sounded like chains being dragged across the floor."

"What did you watch before bed?"

"Golden Girls, like always. That has nothing to do with this."

"There's no ghost. I don't even believe in stuff like that."

"You live in Charleston, and you don't believe in ghosts? We literally have ghost tours here every day."

"Well, I don't buy it. I think it's just something they do for tourists."

"I'm telling you, he's in my attic. I've been feeling like somebody's been up there for the last week or so. Probably the spirit of a Civil War soldier or maybe even a Native American who got the raw end of the deal."

"For reference, I think pretty much all Native Americans got the raw end of the deal."

"Well, whatever! I just know he's up there."

"How do you even know it's a he?"

Willadeene rolled her eyes. "Because a female could never pick up heavy chains like that."

Shelby decided that this argument was probably the most ridiculous she had ever had, so why prolong it?

"I have to get some sleep. I'm working in the morning."

"Well, you go on up. I'm not moving from this spot."

"You can't sleep on the sofa."

"Oh, yes, I can! Unless you have a nice guest room for me?"

"I do not. The only furnished bedroom right now is mine, and I'm sorry, but I need my sleep for work."

"That's just fine with me. I've slept in worse places. Just grab me a quilt and go on to bed."

Shelby could see that she would not win this argument, and she was too tired to continue talking. She grabbed a quilt out of the linen closet and tossed it to Willadeene.

"I have no ghosts over here, so don't come upstairs and scare me to death in the middle of the night."

"Don't worry, I'll leave you alone. But tomorrow I'm calling those ghost hunter people to come check my attic. I'm not living with a ghost for the rest of my life."

Shelby turned off the lights and dragged herself

back up the stairs. Having Willadeene as a neighbor was a full-time job.

The next morning, Shelby could barely get herself down the stairs. She needed coffee, stat. When she walked into her living room, she found Willadeene sacked out on the sofa like she'd been on a bender the night before.

"Willadeene, wake up. I've got to go to work."

For one scary moment, she thought the woman was dead, but Willadeene eventually stirred. "What time is it?"

"Six-thirty."

"Six-thirty! What on earth are you doing awake at this hour?"

"Some of us have to work," Shelby said, walking into the kitchen. She filled the carafe with water and then poured it into her coffee pot, pressing the start button. As she leaned against the counter, her arms crossed, she waited for Willadeene to show up in the kitchen.

"I barely slept last night worrying about that ghost. I don't have the Internet. I need you to find me a ghost hunter and get them out here today," she said, demanding things as soon as she walked into the kitchen.

"I absolutely will not do that. I am already late, and I still have to grab some breakfast. You're just going to have to use the Yellow Pages or something."

Willadeene plopped down onto the barstool. "Come on. I'm an old lady. I just need a phone number." She never seemed to have any problem trying to guilt Shelby into something by using the "old lady" card.

"Again, I'm late for work. Plus, I will not encourage this crazy behavior of thinking you have a ghost in your attic. Are you sure you're not just lonely?"

Willadeene stared at her like she was crazy. "So you think I'm lonely enough that I would get up at two o'clock in the morning and come banging on your door so I could sleep on your uncomfortable sofa? Seriously, that thing should be used for torture."

Shelby had to admit it was an outrageous idea, but anything is possible with Willadeene.

"Fine," Shelby said, pulling her phone from her pocket. Ridiculously, she googled for ghost hunters in the area and found two. She wrote their names and numbers on a piece of paper and gave them to Willadeene. "Now, will you please go home?"

"I'm just going to run in, change my clothes and leave until the ghost hunters can come."

"Can I ask you what it is you think is going to

happen if there is a ghost? I mean, have you ever heard of anybody being murdered by a ghost?"

"Well, no, but there's always a first. I don't have many more years on this planet, but I sure as heck don't wanna go out by ghost murder."

Shelby restrained herself from laughing. She had to give it to Willadeene. She was an interesting soul. And if anybody was going to get murdered by a ghost, it would probably be her. Of course, then she'd just come right back as a ghost herself and taunt Shelby.

Shelby thumbed through the next Jasmine Cain book and swooned. This woman really knew how to write romantic leading men. As handsome and dashing as Reed Sullivan was, these men were even more over the top.

She took a sip of her coffee and read chapter after chapter while she had a lull in the bookstore. Customers had been flooding in all day, most of them picking up the new Jasmine Cain book.

"Hey there," Lacy said as she walked inside. Shelby had never seen her at the bookstore before.

"What a nice surprise. What's up?"

"Well, I needed to chat with you about something."

"Before you do that, I need to ask you something."

"Okay. What is it?"

"I've been reading these books by Jasmine Cain. They're amazing, by the way. Anyway, remember that story you told me about one of your first dates with Ed? Where it rained your picnic out and he danced with you under the stars inside with Frank Sinatra playing?"

She cleared her throat. "Yes, of course."

"Well, that entire scene is word-for-word in this book." She held up the book she'd finished the night before.

Lacy's eyes widened. "Really? What a small world."

"Small world? It was exact. You said you'd never read any of Jasmine Cain's books, right?"

"Nope."

"Well, then you can't have copied it from there. That must mean she somehow heard your story and put it in her book. But how?"

Lacy chuckled. "I believe you're overthinking this. I'm sure I'm not the only woman in the world who had a similar romantic date. Don't worry about it. I'm not giving it a second thought."

"Are you sure you don't know her? Or know somebody who knows her?"

"I'm sure. I appreciate you trying to protect me,

but it's no big deal. I mean, even if the woman knew me and copied my story, I wouldn't be upset."

"I guess so," Shelby said. "So, what did you want to talk to me about?"

Lacy swallowed hard and bit her bottom lip. "It's about Reed."

CHAPTER 13

SHELBY COULDN'T BELIEVE WHAT SHE WAS HEARING. She sat there trying to take it all in, sure that Lacy was mistaken.

"So, you saw Reed and another woman at Waterfront Park last night?"

"Yes. I took the kids there to see the fountain. I turned and saw Reed holding hands with a beautiful young woman. I snuck behind a tree and eavesdropped on their conversation."

"You did? What did he say?"

Lacy pulled out her phone. "I took notes."

"Seriously?" Shelby was both appalled and thankful.

"He told her he loved her and had missed her so much. He also said that she was the most amazing woman he knew, and he never wanted her to leave again. Then he hugged her."

"Did they kiss?"

"Just on the cheek. They just held hands the whole time while they walked. I'm so sorry, Shelby."

She refused to let her eyes fill with tears. This was a new relationship, and it didn't work out. Simple as that. Except she felt shattered inside, and that made her mad at herself for getting so involved. She knew it was too good to be true. Reed Sullivan was a dog, plain and simple.

"I'll be okay," she whispered.

"What are you going to say to him?"

"That I don't care to see him anymore."

"And when he asks for a reason?"

She thought for a moment. "I don't want him to think he ever had the upper hand with me, so I'll tell him I'm not ready for a serious relationship."

"That's always a good excuse to use."

"I guess so."

Lacy reached over and took Shelby's hand. "You deserve so much better than a cheater. I hope you know that."

"I do. And thank you for telling me. Otherwise, I would've looked like a real fool."

Lacy looked at her watch. "Dang it. I need to go pick up Hazel from school. Are you going to be okay?"

Shelby shrugged her shoulders. "Of course. I mean, we haven't been dating all that long, anyway." Inside, her heart was aching. She'd fallen hard for Reed, and it was going to take some time to get over it.

Lacy sat in her car, fingers clenching the steering wheel. Her heart was still pounding from her interaction with Shelby. Not only had she had to tell her about Reed, but she'd had to keep a poker face when Shelby mentioned the book.

Secrets had become the theme of Lacy's life in recent years, and she hated it. She hated having to pretend to be someone she wasn't. She hated having to pretend about her marriage. She hated all of it, and there was no light at the end of that tunnel.

This definitely wasn't what she had planned for her life when she was younger. Lacy had always been open, very social, and not nearly as judgmental as she had become.

Bitterness and resentment would do that to a person.

She loved being a mother, and there was a point in the not so distant past where she had been so proud to be Ed's wife. Now, she didn't really know who she was.

She was keeping two big secrets from her new friends, and it was getting harder by the day. Not necessarily because she was afraid they would find her out, but because she felt like she was lying. She couldn't be her full self without telling them the truth, but she didn't know what people would think of her.

She cared a lot about what people thought, even though she hated that trait in herself. She wanted to be one of those brave people who couldn't care less what other people thought about them, but she wasn't. Image mattered to her.

As she put the key in the ignition and cranked her car, she thought about what could happen if everything came out. What would people think? What would it do to her life? If all of those carefully placed blocks came crashing down, would it crush her life?

Reed had been texting for two days, and Shelby had ignored each one. Then he'd tried calling. She'd ignored that, too. When he came to the bookstore, she was hiding in the back, forcing the little high school girl who worked there part time to do her dirty work and say Shelby wasn't there. Finally, he'd shown up at her front door. She just didn't answer.

She felt like the most immature person on the planet by ignoring him, but she just didn't have the words. If he saw her face, he'd know she was lying about not wanting a relationship. If he heard her voice, he'd hear the quiver just before she was going to cry. She just needed time to get stronger and not care so much about it, but the days were passing with no additional strength being felt.

So, she did the best thing she could think of - left town. Her boss allowed her to take an overnight trip up to Pawley's Island to go to a book signing for Jasmine Cain. Ginger wanted Shelby to convince Jasmine to add Tattered Pages to her book signing schedule. Phone calls and emails had resulted in no answers so far, so Ginger told Shelby to "take the bull by the horns and drive up there".

As she pulled into the parking lot of the book-store on Pawley's Island, she felt a sorrow in her heart. Why would Reed cheat on her? He seemed so interested. Why did men do stuff like that? Of course, women did it too. She was just being a little salty.

She got out of her car and took in a deep breath of the sea air. She wasn't super close to the ocean, but the breeze still made it to the part of the island where the bookstore was. There were lots of people there, a crowd forming outside, making a long single file line all the way down to the hair salon at the end of the small strip of shops.

She got in line, clutching her book to her chest. Even though she wanted to be excited about the book signing and getting to talk to Jasmine Cain, she couldn't get her thoughts off of Reed. There had been so much hope in her heart for that relationship. Now she just felt like she was so clueless that she had fallen for a man who obviously could not be monogamous.

"Are you excited to meet Jasmine Cain?" a woman asked, grinning from ear to ear. She was holding a stack of four books, her blonde ponytail bobbing back-and-forth as they walked up the sidewalk.

"Yes, absolutely," Shelby said, forcing a smile. Any other day, she would've been just as excited. She loved Jasmine's books. But today, she just felt like the wind had been sucked right out of her sails.

"I just love everything she writes. I have all her books. My only wish is that she would write faster!"

"I haven't read all of them, but I'm sure I'll feel the same way soon."

Shelby really wasn't up for small talk. This lady was way too peppy for the early hour, and she just wanted to be left alone. Ginger had asked her to speak to Jasmine, and she hoped that she'd get that chance.

"I just love how she weaves together stories but

then puts some of those steamy scenes in. I fall in love with every man in every book!"

"Well, be careful who you fall in love with, right?" Shelby said, laughing under her breath. The woman stared at her, her head tilted to the side.

"Excuse me?"

"Oh, nothing."

At least it made the woman stop talking to her. They went through the line silently for the next half hour.

Shelby was happy to see when they finally started getting closer to the front of the line. She just wanted to get her book signed, talk to Jasmine, and get back on the road toward Charleston. It was an hour and a half drive, and she wasn't looking forward to it.

Just as she was getting to the front of the line, her phone rang in her pocket. Without thinking, she picked it up and answered it.

"Hello?"

"Shelby, I'm so glad I reached you. I've been worried sick!"

It was Reed. How had she not looked at the caller ID before answering the phone? For a minute, she thought about just hanging up, but that seemed pretty juvenile. Of course, her reaction to the whole thing had been pretty immature overall. She just hated conflict so much.

"No need to worry. I'm perfectly fine," she said in a monotone voice. She didn't want to talk loudly since there were so many people around her.

"I don't understand. I've been trying to reach you for days, even came to your house. I swear, I thought I saw your silhouette in the window. What's going on?"

"Listen, I am on Pawleys Island today at a book signing. I am on a mission from Ginger. I really don't have time to talk about this right now."

"Then when can we talk? This is the first time you've answered my call in several days."

"We'll have to talk later," she said, inching toward the doorway.

"I'll wait at your house."

"No, don't do that, Reed."

"Either we talk now, or I'll be on your doorstep when you get home."

She sighed. "Go in front of me," she whispered to the women behind her as she made her way to the back of the line. "I really don't want to do this right now."

"Shelby, did I do something wrong? I thought things were going really well with us."

She rolled her eyes and laughed. "Yeah, well, so did I."

"Then what happened?"

She didn't want to rat Lacy out, so she decided

not to tell him exactly what Lacy had seen and heard. "Look, after much soul searching, I just decided I'm not ready for a serious relationship right now."

There was a long silence before Reed spoke. "I don't believe you."

"Well, you don't have to. I'm a grown woman, and I can feel how I want to feel."

"Obviously, I've done something to upset you. Let me make it right."

"You can't make anything right, Reed."

"Please talk to me."

The line started moving quickly toward the door. "I have to go now. I have work to do."

"Can I come over tonight?"

"No, Reed. This is over. Please respect my wishes." Without waiting for a response, she ended the call and fought back tears. The last thing she needed was to approach an author they wanted to come to Tattered Pages and look like she was having a nervous breakdown.

There was a woman standing at the door as she approached. "When it's your time, walk to the table and give Jasmine your book. She'll sign it, but she's not allowing pictures today."

"Okay," Shelby said, craning her head to see Jasmine Cain. Her picture wasn't on her books, and

Shelby was curious who this woman was. She needed the distraction right now.

When the sea of people parted, and it was Shelby's turn to walk up to the table, her breath caught in her chest. She just stood there, like a deer in the headlights, staring straight at Jasmine Cain. And Jasmine Cain was staring straight back at her. It was like everybody else around them was frozen in time, and she could no longer hear sounds.

If anyone had told her who would really be sitting behind that table, she would've never believed them.

Cami sat on her sofa, eating a tub of ice cream and staring at the TV. This was her life now. She hadn't been working, hadn't been grooming herself, and had avoided the book club at all costs.

How was this what her life had become? How had she allowed her husband to throw everything off the rails like he had?

The police had been to her house several times, thankfully in unmarked cars so as not to give off any suspicion. One of the hardest things she had ever done was lying to her friends. After all, it was the first set of friends she'd had in a long time.

"I'm going to ask you again. Have you seen Dominic?"

"And I'm going to tell you again that I have not seen him or heard from him since he broke out."

She hated saying those words. How her husband could've broken out of prison was beyond her. Yes, she had told her friends over and over that her husband was this military hero stationed overseas when, in fact, he'd been in prison for years.

Drug offenses, they called them. Dominic had fallen in with the wrong crowd at a very young age, straightened his life out when he met Cami, and then fallen down a dark hole yet again after they were married.

He'd been busted for selling drugs, except he was part of a bigger ring, which meant he was implicated in a lot more than he should've been.

She knew he was guilty. She had never been under the false assumption that her husband was innocent and didn't deserve to go to prison, but it didn't mean that she had stopped loving him or missing him for all those years. But to escape? To run away from his punishment, causing even more grief for her, was beyond anything she thought he'd do.

Thankfully, he hadn't attempted to contact her. She didn't know where he was. She had nothing to tell the police because she was in the dark herself.

For all she knew, he ran across the country and was attempting to start a new life. A part of her was hurt that he didn't contact her, that she wasn't that important. Another part of her was angry that he was adding years to his sentence by trying to escape.

"So you're telling me he hasn't tried to contact you by phone, by text? He hasn't shown up here?"

She took her eyes off the muted TV, which was playing Judge Judy, and stared at the detective. "He might be a criminal, but he's not an idiot. Do you honestly think my husband would break out of prison and then just come home? What kind of moron would do something like that?"

"We're just asking questions, ma'am. We're trying to do our job."

"Well, I don't know where he is. He hasn't contacted me, and he hasn't been here. You're welcome to search the house, top to bottom."

"I appreciate your permission to do just that," he said, nodding at the two other detectives standing near the front door. One went up the stairs and the other one went to the kitchen, probably looking for Dominic in the cabinets.

"For what it's worth, I don't think he should've broken out of prison. I didn't know about his plan."

"I'm sure this is hard for you, but you do under-stand that harboring a fugitive could put you behind bars, right?"

She closed her eyes and laid her head back against the sofa, letting out a big sigh. "Yes, I realize that. I'm not a criminal. I just happened to fall in love with one."

When she'd first met Dominic, he had been clean for a few months. He'd been working at a construction company, and he was making good money. They got married, planned all their future dreams, and then one day while they were eating dinner at a fancy restaurant, Dominic had been arrested right in front of everyone. It was the most embarrassing day of Cami's life.

But she loved him. She saw good in him. When nobody else saw his potential, she did. It was her biggest downfall.

Every day that he had been incarcerated, she'd worried about him. Was he safe? Was he eating? Would he come out of there alive?

He'd had five years left ahead of him, and apparently that was too much. She knew Dominic, and she was well aware that at some point he would try to contact her. And just like all the other days of the last few years, she wondered if he was safe. She wondered if he was eating. But a very tiny part of her never wanted to hear from him again.

~

Shelby couldn't believe her eyes. She slowly walked toward the table with her Jasmine Cain's book in her hand. The woman behind the table was known by a different name to her. Lacy Caldwell.

Lacy's eyes widened like she'd seen a ghost. She forced a smile and held out her hand to take the book, quickly signing it.

"Nice to meet a fan," she said, which was the same thing she had said to so many other people ahead of Shelby.

"Nice to meet one of my favorite authors."

There was a look of begging in her eyes, as if she was asking Shelby not to blow her cover. Shelby didn't, instead turning and walking out of the store and onto the sidewalk. What was it with everybody around her lying lately?

She waited by Lacy's car until the whole event was over. When Lacy came out, she looked like a guilty child who had just gotten caught with her hand in the cookie jar.

"I figured you'd still be here." Morning had turned to afternoon, and Shelby had waited in the hot southern sun to question her neighbor.

"Yeah, I just had a few questions for you. Tattered Pages wanted Jasmine Cain to come to a book signing there. Apparently, you've turned them down quite a few times."

"Actually, I've just ignored their calls and emails. I

can't do a local signing like that. Now you know why."

"Why didn't you tell me? You knew how much I loved these books. You should be proud of your work."

"Can we go have a cup of coffee?"

"Of course."

They walked about half a block to the nearest coffee shop, taking a seat at a small bistro table in the back corner. She was looking around like she was hiding from the FBI.

"I need to tell you some things, and I want to ask you to please keep this information to yourself. As you know, I'm kind of a private person."

"You can trust me."

"Yes, obviously I'm Jasmine Cain. I started writing these books a couple of years ago just as an outlet. My marriage was starting to fall apart, and I'd always wanted to write a novel. I had no idea when I self-published them that they would take off like they did."

"Isn't that a blessing? Something to be proud of?"

"Not when you are the head of the PTA and the coordinator for Vacation Bible School at church. My books are kind of steamy, as you know."

Shelby could see her point. It would've been very hard for people to stomach the kind of books she wrote while she stood up in front of the church or the monthly PTA meeting.

"Sex is a natural thing. Just because you happen to write about it doesn't make you a bad person."

"No, but it certainly wouldn't have instilled confidence in the parents at the PTA meetings. I just didn't want to be the subject of gossip."

"How does your husband feel about your books?"

"For the first year, he didn't know anything about them. He thought I was knitting and crocheting in my hobby room until one day I left my computer open while I changed a diaper. He happened to come home, and I didn't know he was there. He saw everything on the screen, and then he found paperback copies of my books in my desk. He was livid."

"Why?"

"Because he didn't know I was making so much money and funneling it into another account. He thought I was making a plan to leave."

"Why would he think that?"

"Around the time that I started writing the books, my husband cheated on me. I immediately found out, and I set about punishing him."

"Punishing him?"

"Every night after we have dinner as a family, my husband goes to stay in a small apartment he rented. I'll have him come back in the morning and see the kids before school. Other than that, he's not to be in our house."

"Why not just get a divorce?"

"Because I came from a broken home, and I don't want that for my kids."

"Don't you think they'll know, Lacy? When they see their dad in the morning and at dinner, but not at bedtime?"

"I tell them he works odd hours. And he sees them on the weekends at the park."

"That isn't going to work in the long term. You have to know that. Sometimes it's better for the kids if their parents are happy and apart than if they're together and miserable."

"So, you think I can be this divorcee sexy romance author and not have people staring at me in the local grocery store? Gossiping about my cheating husband and steamy book business? I don't want my kids bearing that."

"What if your kids see a strong mother who went after her dreams and succeeded? What if they see a woman who knew her worth and left a relationship that wasn't healthy for her? What if they have two full parents instead of two miserable people pretending to be happy?"

She looked down at her hands, turning her wedding ring on her finger. "When we got married, it was like a fairy tale. We had the same dreams and goals. I never saw the cheating coming."

"We never do," Shelby said, trying not to make the conversation about herself.

Lacy reached over and took her hands. "Thank you for listening to me and keeping my secrets."

"What are you going to do?"

"I have no idea."

CHAPTER 14

"He cheated on you?" Joan said, sitting beside Shelby on her large front porch. Shelby had arrived back from Pawley's Island just before dinnertime. When she saw Joan outside watering her plants, she'd invited her over for a glass of wine.

"It appears so. I can't think of any other reasonable explanation."

"Neither can I. It certainly sounds bad. I'm so sorry, Shelby. I thought y'all were going to be great together."

"So did I."

"Room for one more?" Cami appeared on Shelby's front porch out of nowhere.

"Of course! We've missed you. Are you okay?" Shelby asked, pouring her a glass of wine. Cami sat in one of the black wrought-iron chairs and sighed.

"I'm okay. Just super busy lately. Sorry I missed the last book club meetings. I'll be better the next go round."

"No problem. We just wanted to make sure you were okay."

Cami smiled. "Well, I am. So, what's been going on?"

Shelby quickly filled her in on what Lacy witnessed. Her mouth dropped open. "Oh, honey, I'm so sorry. That's terrible."

"What's terrible?" Lacy asked, walking down the driveway.

"Men!" Shelby yelled, holding her glass of wine in the air. They all laughed.

Lacy poured herself a glass and sat down in the last chair. "Amen to that."

"Trouble in paradise?" Cami asked.

Lacy rolled her eyes. "Paradise is a deserted beach with a hot cabana boy and a line of chocolate cakes that have no calories."

Cami laughed. "I can get on board with that." They all clinked glasses and then sat in silence.

"At the risk of being smacked, I want to say I have a date this weekend," Joan said, smiling slyly.

"A date? Really?" Shelby said.

"Yeah. His name is Randy. I met him at an antique store a few years ago, and he found me on social media. Turns out, he just opened a store near Mount Pleasant."

"Wow, that's amazing, Joan. I'm so happy to see you step back out there. It's courageous," Shelby said.

"It's very courageous and not easy to do," Lacy said, looking at Shelby.

Bam! The sound came from out of nowhere and practically rocked the porch they were sitting on.

"Help! Help!" They all turned around and saw Willadeene running toward them from her house, carrying a skillet in one hand and what appeared to be a handgun in the other. "Call the police!"

"What on earth?" Shelby said, standing up. "What are you doing, Willadeene?"

"He's in my house! Call the cops!"

"Who's in your house?" Cami asked.

Shelby rolled her eyes and sat back down. "She thinks a ghost lives in her attic.

"No! Not a ghost! That man... the convict!"

Shelby stood back up. "He's in your house? Did you shoot him?"

"I think I hit him, but I don't know where. Oh, good Lord, there's probably a dead man in my nice clean kitchen," she said, looking up at the sky and wailing, her arms in the air.

Suddenly, Cami started running toward Willadeene's house. "Dominic! Oh, my gosh! Dominic!"

The women chased behind her as Shelby dialed emergency services.

"Cami, what's happening?" Lacy called, but Cami was running like she was in the Olympics going for the gold medal.

"Did she say Dominic?" Lacy asked as they ran, each of them breathless.

"I think she did," Shelby said back, holding onto her chest so her body parts would stop flapping.

"Why does she know the criminal?" Joan yelled, barely keeping up with them. Although Shelby was impressed that she was a few decades older and making good time as she ran.

When they arrived at Willadeene's front porch, there was a man staggering toward the door, blood on his upper leg. Cami had her arm around him, helping him to a chair.

"Help is coming, honey," she said, her voice soothing.

"I don't want help," he said, trying to stand up. "I've got to get out of here, Cami!"

She pushed him back down into the rocking chair. "No, you don't! You need medical help, Dom. You're bleeding."

"You know what's about to happen, right? They'll take me back to prison and add more time for breaking out. I can't do more time," he said, his voice more like a growl through gritted teeth.

"Why don't we leave you two alone and wait for the medics over there?" Shelby said, ushering everyone toward the street. She knew Cami didn't have much time with the man who must've been her husband.

"Dom, what were you thinking?"

"I was thinking I knew how to break out."

She glared at him. "Not funny. This isn't humorous to me at all."

He pointed to his leg. "You think I think this is funny? That old biddy almost killed me!" It was times like these that his thick, New York accent really came out.

Cami threw her hands in the air. "Well, you know what, Dom? You shouldn't have been hiding out in her attic! She thought she had a ghost!"

He let out a loud laugh. "A ghost? Crazy old lady."

"I'm done with this," she said, sitting down on a nearby bench.

"What do you mean, you're done?"

"Let me be clear, Dominic. *We're* done."

"What? You're leaving me?"

She laughed. "No, you're leaving me. Actually, you left me a long time ago when you chose a life of crime and left me here to be a single wife. I've been devoted to you all this time, and this is how you repay me? Put my neighbor's life in jeopardy? Add more time to your sentence?"

He waved his hand. "You don't mean any of this, Cami. You're just mad right now, but you know we'll make up later." He winked at her the same way he always had.

"No, we won't make up. We can't make up. You're not going to be here. I cannot… No, I will not do this anymore. I deserve a real life, not the fake one I've been living for years now. I made you out to be a military hero, and now my friends know the real gem of a husband I married."

"Friends? Since when do you have friends?"

"Since I joined a book club."

He rolled his eyes. "Oh, jeez, Cami. Really? You're going to dump your husband because of some cackling hens at a book club? Stop being nuts. Help me get outta here before the cops show up." He stood up.

"No."

"No?"

Two police cars raced to the scene and slammed on their brakes right in front of Willadeene's house. Every neighbor on the street was now standing there, staring at Cami and her messed up life. She'd never felt so on display in all her years.

"He's over here, officers," she said loudly as she backed up.

"Cami, come on! Wait for me, baby!"

She shook her head. "No, Dom. This time, I choose myself." With that, she turned around and walked away, listening as he called her name over and over until the police car door slammed and silenced him.

Shelby stared at the bouquet of red roses sitting on her kitchen table. She'd read the card a million times, and a million times her guts had twisted into a knot over it.

Shelby, I miss you. I don't know what I did, but I hope I can fix it. Please call me.

Ugh. Why did relationships have to be so hard? How did he not know what he did? Surely he had to have figured it out by now. Did he think she'd never find out he was cheating on her?

"Coming in! Hope you're decent!" Lacy called as she entered Shelby's home. It had been over a week since the crazy incident with Cami's husband, and tonight was the start of their new book club. They hadn't chosen a book yet, but Shelby had some ideas to pitch to the group.

"No, I'm in the kitchen cooking naked!" Shelby

called back, laughing. Even though her heart was broken, she was glad to have her friends. They were all so different, but they just meshed well together.

She had never thought they would all become such close friends, but they had. She knew that she could count on these women for support, and that meant everything to her.

"Hello?" Joan called from the front door.

"Come on in!" Shelby and Lacy called out simultaneously.

Joan joined them in the kitchen. "I brought homemade chicken salad."

"Oh, that sounds good," Shelby said, taking the bowl from her and putting it on the island.

"Do we know if Cami is coming tonight?" Joan asked.

"I haven't heard from her in the last few days. I know she's been dealing with a lot of emotions."

"How could she not? I mean, the end of a marriage is a huge thing," Lacy said, cutting her eyes at Shelby.

"Very true," Shelby responded.

"Where do I put this?" Willadeene suddenly appeared in the kitchen, a casserole dish in her hand. "It's a cheesy broccoli casserole with black olives."

Lacy stared at Shelby and mouthed, "*with black olives?*" Shelby shrugged her shoulders.

"Right over there," Shelby said, smiling at Lacy.

"How are you doing after the whole escaped prisoner escapade?"

Willadeene sighed. "It was scary to know that man was living in my attic while I was in the house, but honestly, I'm more worried about Cami. I do hope she's okay."

Lacy walked over and felt Willadeene's forehead. "Are you feeling okay?"

Willadeene swiped her hand away. "Very funny."

"I think it's very nice that you're worried about Cami," Shelby said. There was hope, after all.

"Sorry I'm a bit late." They all turned to see Cami standing in the doorway of the kitchen, holding two bottles of wine. "I figured I'd bring these over so I don't drown my sorrows alone at home."

Lacy took them. "Good idea."

"How are you doing?" Shelby asked.

Cami sat on one of the bar stools. "I cried for the first two days. Literally, I never stopped crying. My eyes were red and swollen, and I think I got dehydrated. Or maybe it was the wine I was drinking, too."

"Oh, honey," Joan said, reaching over and patting her hand.

"Now I'm just a bit numb, you know?"

"Are you going to give him another chance?" Lacy asked.

Cami shook her head. "No. Absolutely not. That

part of my life is over. I deserve a man who's actually here with me. I deserve someone who thinks of me first."

"That's exactly right. I'm glad you figured that out," Willadeene said. Cami looked surprised at her comment, but let it pass.

"So, should we get started with the meeting? I hate to keep everyone waiting," Cami said. There were some new women in the living room, and Shelby wanted to get to know them better, too.

"Sure."

Everyone got settled in the living room, and Shelby stood in front of the fireplace to speak. "I'd like to welcome everyone to the Waverly Lane Book Club. This is our second session, and we had so much fun last time! We haven't chosen a book yet…"

Lacy stood up. "Excuse me, Shelby. I'd like to speak, if you don't mind?"

Shelby was thrown off guard, but nodded and sat down. "Go right ahead."

Lacy cleared her throat and stood there silently for a moment before finally speaking. "For so many years, I've portrayed myself to be this perfect wife and mother. I've judged others for not living up to those standards as well. I'm sorry for not being real and authentic."

"What's she talking about?" Cami whispered to Shelby.

"My marriage fell apart years ago, but I wasn't willing to admit it or let other people see what it had become. The truth is that my husband cheated on me, and instead of going to counseling or getting a divorce, I decided to punish him. I didn't want my kids to come from a broken home, but if I'm being honest, I didn't want my reputation to suffer. Embarrassingly, I think that took precedence even over my kids."

"Did you know all of this?" Cami leaned over to ask Shelby. Shelby nodded slightly and then looked back at Lacy.

"So, I forced my husband to get an apartment and leave every night. He would come back in the morning to see the kids off to school, go to work, come to dinner to pretend everything was okay, and then go back to his apartment. To be honest, my plan was for this to continue for the next sixteen years until all of my kids were adults. I know it sounds completely insane, but it seemed logical in my mind at the time."

"Sixteen years? Did I hear that right?" Willadeene asked, leaning over to Shelby.

"I was able to get my husband to agree to this because the person he cheated with happens to be his boss's wife. I threatened to tell his boss and cause him to lose his potential to become a partner. But there was another secret that I was also keeping."

"There's more?" Cami asked, again leaning over to Shelby.

"I've been writing books under the name Jasmine Cain for the last couple of years. They became really popular, but I didn't want anybody to know it was me."

"Why? That sounds like a great accomplishment," Joan said.

"Because Jasmine Cain writes steamy novels."

"*You* write steamy books?" Cami said, her mouth hanging open.

"I do. And I do it very well. I make more than enough income to support myself and the kids without my husband, although I'm going to hit him for alimony with everything I've got," she said, smiling.

"Wait, so you're getting divorced?" Cami asked.

"Yes. I'm tired of hiding who I am. I'm tired of keeping secrets from my friends. I filed for divorce yesterday. My husband will be getting joint custody because it's very important that the kids have two happy parents who love them. We've worked all of that out. Now for the alimony, and then we'll be all done," she said, grinning from ear to ear.

"Why did you decide to tell us all of this?" Willadeene asked.

"Like I said, I'm tired of hiding. I think I deserve better. I deserve a man who won't cheat on me. And my kids deserve an authentic mother who isn't keeping all these secrets. I'm coming out of the shadows as Jasmine Cain. I'm proud of the talent I have for writing great novels that just happen to have a little steaminess mixed into them. And that's why I wanted to ask if you ladies might be interested in reading one of my books as our next selection?"

Shelby was surprised that Lacy had suggested that. This was a complete turnaround she wasn't expecting.

"I think that's a great idea! I've already read the books, and you won't be able to put them down!" Shelby said, looking around at everybody.

"I'm game!" Cami said, Joan nodding as well. Everybody in the room was in agreement except for Willadeene, who sat there with a scowl on her face.

"Willadeene, what do you think?" Shelby asked.

"I'm not reading pornography."

Shelby started laughing. "It's not like that at all. These are beautifully written novels that have a little extra spice to them."

"Well, I guess I'll give it a try. But if it makes me uncomfortable, I'll just throw that book right in the trashcan!"

Lacy laughed. "I would expect nothing less, Willadeene."

~

As Lacy drove down the road toward Graystone to pick up her lunch, she felt such a wave of relief in her body. All the years of tension that she had been holding in her neck and shoulders seemed to disappear overnight. Telling her kids, in an age appropriate way, that their parents were divorcing was hard, but she thought she had done a good job with it.

Now it was time for her to build her own life away from her husband as an independent woman. Maybe she would fall in love again one day, but that was the furthest thing from her mind. Right now, she just wanted to raise her kids, be an involved parent, and write her books. She felt like she was able to come out of the proverbial closet and show everybody who she really was. And if they judged her, so be it.

She walked into Graystone and up to the hostess stand, and waited for the woman to ask her name. Instead, she was surprised to see a very tired-looking Reed Sullivan walk toward her.

"Oh, Reed. I wasn't expecting to see you here during the day."

"I'm pretty much here all the time right now. I need a distraction. I'm sure you've heard that Shelby has stopped speaking to me for some reason."

"I've heard."

"You wouldn't know anything about that, would you?"

"No, I wouldn't."

"Why do I think you're lying to me about that?"

"Because I am."

"Lacy, I really don't know what I did to deserve this. I thought Shelby and I were on the right track. I could feel myself falling in love with her."

"Then maybe you shouldn't have cheated."

His face looked like he had seen a ghost. Literally all the color drained out of it, and his mouth dropped open. "What?"

"Come on, Reed. Don't try to play dumb. I heard everything, and I saw it with my own two eyes."

"What are you talking about?"

"I was over at Waterfront Park when I saw you holding hands with another woman. You hugged her, kissed her on the cheek. You told her how much you had missed her, how amazing she was, how much you loved her."

He put his face in his hands and growled. "Oh, my gosh. Is that what all of this has been about? You told Shelby that I was cheating on her?"

"I know what I saw. And being a woman who was just cheated on, I know what that looks like." She took her bag from the counter and turned toward the door. "Leave Shelby alone. She's not the kind of woman you cheat on."

She walked out the door and got into her car, Reed calling after her the entire time.

Shelby stood atop the stepladder on her tiptoes. She always hated putting books on the very top shelves. She had the worst balance of anyone she knew, so she had a very hard time not falling off. Bracing herself with her left foot on the shelf and her right foot on the ladder, she reached as high as she could to put three books on the top.

Just as she placed the books, she somehow started to lose her balance and fell backwards. Knowing that she was about to hit the table below, she waited for her life to flash before her eyes. Isn't that what was supposed to happen?

Instead, she fell into something soft. Something warm. Something familiar.

She turned her head and noticed she had fallen into Reed Sullivan's arms. Where did he even come from? She didn't hear the front door open, which meant that he had to have been in the shop for quite a while.

Psycho, she thought. *Stalker*. But she was also thankful he saved her from breaking her back.

"Put me down, please."

He slowly lowered her to the ground until she

was on her feet. Instinctively, she took her hands and ran them down the front of her clothes as if she was trying to get the wrinkles out.

"You scared me to death. You could've really hurt yourself. Why on earth would you be up there alone?"

"Well, apparently I wasn't alone. How long have you been stalking me around the store?"

"I wasn't stalking you, Shelby. I guess you just didn't hear the door chime."

That was possible. She often got lost in thought when she was doing other things, especially when all she could think about was Reed.

"What do you want? I've asked you to leave me alone, so unless you are in dire need of a specific book, you really shouldn't be here. "

"I'm here because Lacy came to Graystone to pick up lunch, and she told me the reason you haven't been speaking to me."

She walked past him back to the counter. "Well, if she told you, it wasn't her place to tell."

"Since she's the one who gave you the wrong information, she definitely was the one who should've told me. Actually, you should've told me, too."

She stared at him. "You're blaming this on me? The fact that you cheated when we had just started dating?"

"I didn't cheat! That whole situation isn't what you think it was."

"Everybody says that when they get caught."

"Shelby, that was my sister."

"What?"

"That was my sister, Leanne. I hadn't seen her in several years because she had a falling out with my parents. She reached out to me and said she was in town and asked if I could meet her at Waterfront Park."

"I didn't know you had a sister."

"We hadn't gotten around to those conversations yet. But that was Leanne. I did tell her that I loved her and that she's amazing and that I missed her. I did hold her hand, give her a hug, and give her a kiss on the cheek. But I can guarantee I didn't cheat on you with my sister."

Shelby felt like the world's biggest fool. She should've talked to him instead of cutting him off completely and not even giving him an opportunity to explain.

"I'm so sorry," Shelby said, covering her face. She was completely embarrassed.

"I just wish you would've talked to me. I can't be in a relationship with somebody who shuts me out like that. I thought we really had something special."

"I thought so, too. I've been devastated."

"I don't understand what I did to deserve you not even giving me a chance to tell you about my sister."

"I don't know what to say."

He walked closer and leaned against the other side of the counter. "I've been single all these years because I couldn't find the right partner. I thought I might have had that in you, Shelby."

"I thought that, too. But I understand if you don't want to see me anymore because the way I handled everything was pretty immature. Once I shut you out, I felt like I had to dig in my heels no matter what."

"I agree. It was immature. But we all do things that are immature from time to time."

"Does that mean you want to see me again?" she asked, slightly smiling as butterflies zipped around her stomach.

He pulled on her hand until she came out from behind the counter and faced him. "I'd like to see you every day, Shelby. But from now on, please give me a chance to explain if you're mad at me, okay?"

"Will do, but I'd rather not be mad at you," she said, laughing.

"Is this the part where we make up? Because I was really looking forward to that," he said, winking at her.

She reached up and pulled his face toward hers. "I guess we can do that."

EPILOGUE

Six Months Later

Shelby finished icing the cake and pulled the casserole from the oven. Today was going to be so much fun, but she was an anxious wreck, trying to make it all come together.

"Did you finish icing it?" Lacy asked as she breezed back into the kitchen. Lacy was a godsend with party planning, cooking, and baking. She'd thrown so many dinner parties for her ex-husband that she could practically do them with her eyes closed.

"I did."

Lacy looked at it and laughed. "Honey, you missed a whole chunk over here." She grabbed the knife and took care of it herself. Lacy was now a divorced mother, but she was doing so well. She was writing more books, and had just signed a new seven-figure publishing contract. Shelby was so happy for her.

"My brain is fried. Do you think he knows?"

"No. Men are generally clueless, I've found," Lacy said, already moving over to the pitcher of lemon-ade. She stirred it and breezed back out into the dining room.

"I finished the balloons and got the banner hung," Joan said, walking into the kitchen. "It looks so festive out there!"

"Thank you so much, Joan. You've been a tremendous help. Where's Cami?"

"She just finished teaching her yoga class, but she's walking across the street right now. And Randy will be coming in a bit." Joan and Randy had been dating for almost six months, and Shelby was so happy to see Joan smiling and in love. She assumed they'd eventually tie the knot. Joan had mended fences with her son too, which was wonderful because that meant she got to be a grandma to little Andy.

As for Cami, she was also newly divorced and trying to make a better life for herself. She had adopted an adorable boxer dog from the shelter, and she was looking at renting her own space to teach yoga. The business opportunity she was so excited about when Shelby met her had fallen by the wayside somewhere along the way.

"When is this shindig going to start?" Willadeene asked so loudly that Shelby could hear her across the house.

"When he gets here!" Shelby called back. Willadeene was definitely an acquired taste. She was ornery and often belligerent, but she was their friend by some weird miracle.

The women of Waverly Lane all took care of each other. Nobody was alone, and they stuck together. Shelby was thankful for Gigi's idea of starting a book club, because it had definitely changed her life for the better.

Shelby and Reed had gotten more serious over the last six months. She felt like she knew more about him than she had learned about her ex-husband in over a decade. She felt safe and comfortable with him, and there wasn't a doubt in her mind that her dating days were over. If she didn't marry Reed Sullivan one day, she'd just be an old maid because they didn't make men any better than him.

"He's driving down the street!" Lacy yelled from the front door. "Everybody hide!"

Shelby ran out of the kitchen and into the living room, ready to surprise Reed for his birthday. Instead, all her friends were facing her, smiling.

"What's going on? Don't we need to hide?" Everybody was grinning from ear to ear, and Lacy was already wiping her eyes. Shelby was utterly confused. "Where is Reed?"

The crowd parted, and she saw Reed down on one knee, his eyes welling with tears and a small blue ring box in his hand.

"Hey, Shelby."

"What's happening?" A part of her knew what was happening, but the larger part of her couldn't believe it.

"I know it's only been six months, but it's been the best six months of my life. I'm tired of being Charleston's oldest bachelor." Everybody laughed. "Would you do me the honor of being my wife for the rest of my life?"

He flipped open the box showcasing the most beautiful, yet tasteful, princess cut engagement ring she'd ever seen. "I don't know what to say…"

"Try saying yes!" Willadeene yelled out. Again, everyone laughed.

"I'd appreciate that," Reed replied, smiling.

"Yes!" Shelby yelled, jumping up and down. "Of course, it's yes!"

Reed stood, put the ring on her finger, and hugged her tightly. Shelby had never felt the type of joy and love she felt in that moment.

"I love you, Shelby Anderson," he said, pressing his lips against her neck.

"I love you too, Reed Sullivan, my soon-to-be husband."

And she loved the family she'd built on Waverly Lane. It really was a good life.

Want to find out about new releases and giveaways? Go to www.RachelHannaAuthor.com and join my newsletter and private Facebook reader group!

Made in United States
North Haven, CT
03 November 2022

26243909R00146